'Don't you have somewhere else you need to be?' Alice asked as she knelt back down at her station.

'The nurses will look for me if they need me. It seems to me, though, you could do with some help here.'

They worked together as the sun continued to beat down. The women and the men sang as they mixed mud and pounded their bricks.

Dante smiled to himself as he watched Alice leave the brick-making, only to return a short while later carrying a load of wood on her back. Her hair was mussed up and she had a smear of dirt across her nose, but she had never looked more beautiful to him. He had been badly mistaken thinking she was some spoilt princess. The woman who worked here and had won the admiration of the camp was the same woman who had driven him crazy with longing back in Italy.

Alice threw the wood to the ground with an explosion of breath.

'I'll never complain about the gym again,' she muttered. But she smiled at him, and it was as if the sun had come from behind a cloud. Her eyes were sparkling like the sun on water.

Dear Reader

Tuscany is one of my favourite parts of the world, and some readers will know that Africa is also very close to my heart. In this book I have brought these two places together as my hero and heroine learn about themselves and each other.

Alice meets the gorgeous and dangerously sexy Dr Dante Corsi in Florence, and has a brief but intense affair with him. But Dante doesn't know that Alice is keeping a secret from him. She is not the woman he thinks she is, but is Lady Alice Granville, daughter of one of the richest men in England.

When Dante discovers the truth, and that Alice is planning to come to work as a volunteer in Africa, where he works as one of the camp doctors, he is dismayed. Not only does he not believe she will be able to cope with the harsh conditions of camp life, but he has sworn not to let her back into his heart.

As they work together Dante learns that, despite her high heels and manicured nails, Alice is determined to make herself useful, and she is soon an essential part of the camp—and his life.

But can he trust this woman? And, even if he can, does he have the right to take her away from her privileged life? Can Alice make him believe in love again?

I hope you enjoy finding out.

Best wishes

Anne Fraser

THE DOCTOR AND THE DEBUTANTE

BY
ANNE FRASER

GW 31818781

First published in Great Britain 2011
by Mills & Boon, an imprint of Harlequin (UK) Limited.
Large Print edition 2011
Harlequin (UK) Limited, Eton House,
18-24 Paradise Road, Richmond, Surrey TW9 1SR

© Anne Fraser 2011

ISBN: 978 0 263 21765 0

Printed and bound in Great Britain
by CPI Antony Rowe, Chippenham, Wiltshire

Anne Fraser was born in Scotland, but brought up in South Africa. After she left school she returned to the birthplace of her parents, the remote Western Islands of Scotland. She left there to train as a nurse, before going on to university to study English Literature. After the birth of her first child she and her doctor husband travelled the world, working in rural Africa, Australia and Northern Canada. Anne still works in the health sector. To relax, she enjoys spending time with her family, reading, walking and travelling.

Recent titles by the same author:

DAREDEVIL, DOCTOR…DAD!†
PRINCE CHARMING OF HARLEY STREET
RESCUED: MOTHER AND BABY
MIRACLE: MARRIAGE REUNITED
SPANISH DOCTOR, PREGNANT MIDWIFE*

†*St Piran's Hospital*
**The Brides of Penhally Bay*

To Lisa, for showing me the real Italy.
Mille grazie, bella.

PROLOGUE

ALICE picked up her pencil and made a few more strokes on her pad. Somehow her depiction of Michelangelo's *David* wasn't going according to plan. In her drawing he looked more like the Incredible Hulk than one of the world's masterpieces.

She had come to the Piazza della Signoria as soon as it was light so that she would be there before the tourists. Florence was teeming with them and it wasn't really surprising that the Italian city was so popular, it was an art lover's dream. Everywhere Alice looked there were statues, stunning architecture and amazing works of art that she'd only ever read about. Only yesterday she had seen the original statue of Michelangelo's *David* and had been moved to tears. Now she was here in the square to sketch the copy.

Even at eight o'clock in the morning the square was filling rapidly. She decided to give it another hour before packing up.

Picking up her pencil again, she sighed with pleasure as the sun warmed her skin. This was the first time she'd been truly content for as long as she could remember. Here in Florence she could be anonymous, nobody knew or cared who she was and that suited her just fine. There were no paparazzi ready to leap out at her to snap a photograph that would be splashed all over the next day's gossip magazines. No dinners or functions to attend. No home to run. For these, all-too-short three weeks, she was simply Alice Granville.

She held her pad at arm's length and surveyed it critically. She wasn't much of an artist and never would be, but she was bored with hanging about the villa and wanted to record some of the great stuff she had seen. When she'd finished here she'd go and have a coffee and one of those delicious pastries at a café. It was her daily treat. The trouble was that she liked food. Every time she passed a pastry shop, Alice would look longingly at the display in the window—and unfortunately Florence had them on practically every street corner—noticing yet another type of cake she simply had to try.

The Italians also loved their food but Alice had to be careful—just one look at all the delicious food and she felt her hips expand. Not that she was really overweight, just more curvy than she would have liked.

She was about to pack up her bag when her eyes were drawn to a figure sitting on a bench opposite her.

Dressed in a pair of thigh-hugging faded blue jeans and a white T-shirt with the sleeves cut off, the man was muscular without being bulky. His face was turned upwards as if he was drinking in the rays of the sun. The muscles of his arms rippled as he lifted his arms and pulled his T-shirt over his head. Alice took a deep breath. He was a real-life copy of the statue of Michelangelo she had been attempting to draw. His chest and arms were tanned and fine dark hair formed a V down to the top button of his jeans.

She started to sketch his face. Dark, almost black hair flopped across a broad forehead. He had a long Roman nose and a strong jawline.

She moved to the mouth: full lips, the edges turned up at the corner as if he was a man who was used to laughing. As if he could read her mind, he smiled, stretched and opened eyes framed by eyelashes that were longer than hers. His eyes were not quite brown with a glint that made them almost amber. Perfectly straight white teeth. Of course. This man couldn't possibly have an imperfection. He was without a doubt the most beautiful man she had seen in real life—and that was saying something.

As she ran her eyes over his chest, her pencil scribbling furiously on the paper, she saw that he wasn't perfect. Across his chest was a scar. A few inches long, it ran in a diagonal line from his shoulder down towards his abdomen.

Alice took a long swig of tepid water. For some reason her mouth was dry.

The man shifted slightly before lifting his T-shirt from the bench beside him. As he raised his arms to put it back on, his muscles bunched.

Alice fanned herself with a piece of paper from her pad. Florence was hot in midsummer.

Ten more days and she'd be going back to her life in London. She sighed. Why did the thought fill her with dread? Most women would give their eye teeth to live her life. But to her it felt empty, almost pointless. On the other hand, since she'd come to Italy she'd had the strange sense of coming home. It was crazy. She could barely speak the language and as far as she knew there were no Italians in her ancestry. Perhaps it was because here she could be anonymous Alice instead of Lady Alice Granville, daughter of one of the richest men in London.

For once in her life, Alice wasn't on show and she intended to make the most of it. Every morning she left the villa and wandered around Florence, drinking in the art and architecture, craning her neck lest she miss another breathtaking sculpture or carving. She'd promised Peter that she would think about his proposal. In every way he should be the right man for her. He was perfect husband material—wealthy, sophisticated, aristocratic and, even more importantly as far as her father was concerned, he had a bright future with her father's company. But, and this was a big but, he did nothing to set Alice's heart racing. In fact, 'boring' was the word that sprang to mind. She had come to Florence to give herself time and space to think about his proposal and already she knew she could never marry him. Telling him would be awful, but she would do it as soon as she got home.

This last week and a half, Alice had allowed herself to daydream that she was Italian, an ordinary woman living an ordinary life, and she liked the feeling. For the rest of her time in Italy she was going to be Alice Granville, university student, who had to bring her lunch into the city to save money. Even if that lunch was provided by the trained chef who worked at her father's friend's holiday villa.

A screech of brakes and a terror-filled scream

filled the air, jerking her out of her reverie. For a moment there was silence as the world seemed to stop. Alice jumped up, abandoning her belongings on the step and hurried over to where the noise had come from.

At first it was difficult to see what had happened. A jumble of metal and clothes lay on the ground where one of the stalls selling leather handbags had been knocked over. Next to it was a moped, its wheels twisted and the metal bent and misshapen. A car had careered off to one side and as they watched a man staggered out of the car. He swayed and clutched the bonnet of his car for support.

'*Dio mio*,' he said, shocked and dazed. '*Dio mio.*'

Horrified, Alice spotted the still form of a little girl lying on the ground. A few feet from her, a woman was moaning and struggling to sit up.

The man from the bench was running towards the victims and without thinking Alice followed him.

'*Chiamante un ambulanza!*' he shouted to the

people who had stopped to stare as he dropped to his knees beside the injured girl. A young woman instantly punched numbers into a phone. Everyone else was still staring in horrified silence. Some even began to move away.

'Can I help?' Alice asked, dropping to her knees beside the man she had been sketching only minutes before.

'Go to the woman,' he replied in accented English. 'Make sure she stays still and that no one else tries to move her until I have examined her. I need to see to the child first.' He must have noticed Alice's hesitation. '*Prego!* Go!' he said. 'I'm a doctor. I'll be there as soon as I can.'

Her heart thumping, Alice ran across to the woman. She hoped she wasn't badly injured. The only experience of first aid Alice had was a course she had taken at school and that had been four years ago. At least the woman was conscious and breathing. Wishing she could speak Italian, Alice spoke quietly to the grey-haired victim, hoping that the woman would at least be reassured by her presence. She mumbled something that Alice couldn't follow. Fortunately the woman who had phoned for the ambulance stopped and translated. 'She is asking if her grandchild is okay,' she told Alice.

'Tell her a doctor is looking at her now.'

The grandmother started to raise herself off the ground. Alice pressed her back, gently but firmly. 'No, no. You mustn't move till the doctor's examined you. You could make any injuries you do have worse.' While her words were hurriedly translated, Alice searched for signs of injury. She winced in sympathy as she noticed that the grandmother's ankle looked to be broken.

'You'll be fine. An ambulance is on its way.'

The grandmother's gaze was straining towards her granddaughter, who was partly obscured by the kneeling doctor. The woman muttered another stream of incomprehensible Italian.

'A prayer,' the bystander told Alice.

Alice stood to see if she could help the driver of the car.

His forehead was bleeding profusely, but Alice had read somewhere that even shallow head wounds tended to do that. Apart from the cut to his head and his dazed expression he didn't seem badly hurt. 'I didn't see them. I was talking on my phone. I didn't see them.'

'Someone has phoned for an ambulance,' Alice reassured him. 'They will be here soon.'

'Could you stay with this lady and this gentleman?' Alice asked the helpful bystander. 'I'll be back in a minute. I must see if the doctor needs help.'

Her heart still beating painfully fast, Alice sped across to where the doctor was examining the child. Alice noticed that he'd moved the little girl into the recovery position. She was disturbingly pale but what was worse was that she had a piece of metal protruding from just below her collar bone. Horrified, Alice sucked in a breath. The man had removed his T-shirt and was using it to staunch the blood pumping from the wound.

Although his attention was focussed on his patient, he must have sensed her presence.

'Are the other two all right?' he asked.

'The driver seems okay, but the grandmother seems to have broken her ankle.'

'What is your name?'

'Alice.'

'I am Dante. I need you to help me so I can check the other patients, Alice,' he said. He guided her hand towards the pumping wound. 'Press here as firmly as you can. Don't stop applying pressure whatever happens.'

Gingerly Alice did as she was asked. She didn't want to hurt the child any more than necessary. The bleeding increased.

Immediately an impatient hand was on top of hers again, pressing the pad into the wound. '*Dio mio*, did I not say *firmly*?' he growled. 'We want to stop the blood, not mop it up!'

'Okay. I get it. I get it.'

His dark gaze held hers for a split second. Then he released his hold and turned away. Over the buzzing of the audience around them, Alice heard the voice of the child's grandmother calling out to the little girl.

Within seconds the makeshift bandage was

soaked with blood. Alice was aware of the sound of the child's grandmother's distress above the noise of the traffic.

As if aware of her grandmother's cries, the little girl's eyes flickered.

Alice leaned forward and spoke softly to her. 'It's okay, sweetheart. Try to stay as still as you can.' She kept her voice low and managed a smile.

Dante laid his head on the girl's chest. 'I wish I had my stethoscope. As far as I can make out her breathing is okay, but she needs to get to hospital.'

'Shouldn't we try and remove the metal from her shoulder?' Alice asked.

'No, absolutely not. If we did that we could make matters worse. Much worse.'

'Really?' The makeshift bandage was ominously soaked with blood.

'Really,' he repeated. 'Stay with the little one while I check her grandmother. Keep talking to her. Whatever you do, keep the pressure on her wound. I'll be back as soon as I can. Call me if there is any change.'

Alice could only nod. Her heart was banging so hard against her ribs it was almost painful. She didn't want to be left in charge of the child. What if her condition changed suddenly? Alice knew she wouldn't have a clue what to do.

'Nonna?' the child whispered.

'The doctor is looking after your *nonna*. What's your name?'

'Sofia.'

'Okay, Sofia. Can you understand English?'

'A little bit. I am learning at school.'

'Everything's going to be just fine. Soon the ambulance will be here to take you to hospital. In the meantime, you have to lie as still as you can. Will you do that?'

The child nodded. Alice kept her eyes fixed on the little girl's and made herself smile reassuringly.

'I hurt. I want my *mamma*.' The child was beginning to panic. Alice knew she had to keep her from moving. She placed a hand on the child's shoulder and glanced around. Dante was bent over Sofia's grandmother.

'Where is your *mamma*?' Alice asked.

'She's at home. Nonna and I shop for food.'

'Where do you live?' Alice wanted to keep the child's attention from what was happening a few feet away.

'Back up the road. In the mountains. I help my *nonna*.'

'Your mama must be proud of you. And she'll be even prouder when she hears what a brave girl you've been.'

To Alice's relief, the wail of an approaching ambulance cut through the sound of traffic. At last help was on its way. She looked over her shoulder. Dante was still occupied with the child's grandmother but, as if sensing her eyes on him, he looked up from whatever he was doing and raised a questioning eyebrow. Alice nodded to let him know that the child was okay.

'Come with me. In the ambulance?' the little girl asked. 'I'm scared.'

Alice squeezed her hand. 'Of course. And I'll stay until your *mamma* and *papà* come, if you like.'

Sofia dipped her head slightly, then, to Alice's relief, Dante was by her side again. The ambulance was getting closer but by the sound it had become snarled in traffic.

'How is she doing?' Dante asked.

'Okay, under the circumstances. She's conscious and speaking.'

Dante pulled out his mobile phone and said something to Sofia in Italian.

Sofia whispered a number and Dante punched the numbers into the phone and moved away still keeping a close eye on the injured child. Alice guessed he was calling Sofia's parents and she didn't envy him his task. She could only imagine how the mother would feel when she heard about the accident.

As he was speaking the ambulance drew up and a couple of paramedics jumped out. While one stayed to check over the driver of the car, the other ran towards them. Alice continued to hold the young girl's hand as the paramedic set about putting up a drip. Dante finished the call and his shoulders slumped. He crossed back to them and updated the paramedic in rapid Italian.

Within minutes, Sofia was being loaded into the ambulance. Alice understood enough to know that another ambulance was on its way to collect the grandmother.

'I'm going with her,' Alice told Dante. 'I promised I would.'

Dante nodded and helped her into the back of the ambulance. '*Bene*. She will be less frightened with a familiar face. I am coming too.' He lowered his voice. 'There is still a chance she could collapse. She's lost a lot of blood.'

At the hospital, Dante went with the other doctors as they rushed Sofia away behind some doors. Left alone, Alice found a chair and sat down. She couldn't bear to leave, not until she knew for sure that Sofia was going to be okay. When she looked at her watch she was amazed to find that only an hour and a half had passed since the accident. Although desperately worried for the little girl, Alice experienced a gratifying sense of achievement. It had felt good helping and she hadn't been squeamish at all at the sight of blood—at least, not after her first sight of the wound. She had surprised herself by staying calm and not panicking.

Another hour passed before she looked up to find Dante standing next to her. Immersed in her thoughts she hadn't heard him approach. He had changed out of his clothes and was wearing blue hospital scrubs. If anything he looked more handsome than when she'd first seen him on the park bench. The thin cotton material emphasised the breadth of his chest and his powerful thighs. In the hospital environment he was even more assured, as if this was where he belonged.

'Sofia is going to be okay. The surgeons managed to remove the metal from her shoulder. Luckily it hadn't torn any major blood vessels so she should be able to go home in a day or so.' He smiled down at her. 'You did a good job back there, Alice.' She liked the way he said her name. It made her feel interesting, exotic even.

'I was terrified at first,' she admitted. 'But since Sofia had much more reason to be scared than I had, I couldn't let her see my fear. I'm so glad she's going to be okay.

Alice shivered.

Dante picked up a blanket from one of the benches and wrapped it gently around her shoulders. 'You have had a shock.' He sat down next to her. 'I am going to wait until Sofia's parents get here, but you should go back to your hotel. Do you wish me to call you a taxi?'

'No, that's all right,' Alice said. 'I just need a moment.'

Now the adrenaline was draining away, Alice felt exhausted. She leant her head against the wall and closed her eyes. Despite everything, she was acutely conscious of Dante. The skin on her upper arms tingled where his fingertips had brushed against her skin and she could almost feel the heat of his body next to her. Although his presence was disconcerting the silence that fell between them was comfortable. She was curious to know more about this man.

It had been a huge relief to discover he was a doctor but it had also been a surprise. Out of all the jobs she'd imagined he'd do, medicine wasn't one of them. Now if he'd been a model or a professional footballer, somehow *that* would have seemed more believable.

'What kind of doctor are you?' she asked.

'I am a children's doctor. How do you say it?'

'A paediatrician.'

'*Sì*, a paediatrician.' he held out his hands as if in explanation. They were long fingered and smooth. An image of his hands on her bare skin flashed unbidden into Alice's head and she flushed.

'I saw you in the square,' Dante said. 'You were drawing. Are you an artist?'

Alice felt her face getting redder. Had he noticed she was sketching him? She hoped to hell not.

'If you saw my pictures you would know I'm not an artist.'

'Is that your notebook?' He pointed to her handbag where, sure enough, her notepad was peeking out of her bag. 'Can I see it?' Before she could stop him he had reached in and plucked it out of bag. Resisting the impulse to grab it out of his hands, she nodded when he raised a questioning eyebrow.

Flushed with embarrassment, she waited while he flicked through her drawings. With a bit of luck he wouldn't recognise himself. It wasn't as if her sketch bore much relation to the real thing. It wasn't much good and it certainly didn't do credit to the real man.

But when he paused at the last page and grinned she knew her hopes had been in vain.

'I didn't know I looked like that,' he said seriously, but she could hear the laughter in his voice.

Double damn. She peered over her shoulder. Her sketch was out of proportion, the figure listing to one side. Never mind. It wasn't as if she wanted to make a career as an artist.

'You don't. You're much better…' Just in time, Alice bit back the rest of the words. 'I mean I'm not very good at drawing,' she said. 'It's only a hobby.' She took the pad from him and replaced it in her bag.

'What is it you do when you are not drawing?' he asked her.

Now there was the rub. She was reluctant to tell him that she acted as a social secretary for her father, his hostess whenever he was between girlfriends, that apart from her studies she didn't actually do anything except run Granville House and attend lunches and dinners. Not that any of that was easy. Moreover, she had promised herself that she would be plain Alice while she was here and she saw no need to tell this stranger who she really was.

'I'm a student in London. Studying History of Art.' That much she could tell him.

'Then you are a visitor in my city. You like it so far?' He smiled at her and her heart did a little somersault.

'I love it. It's so beautiful. The history, the art—' she wasn't going to mention the pastry shops '—the lifestyle. I can tell you after a pretty miserable, wet summer in England it is heaven to feel the sun.'

Dante's eyebrows shot up and her heart did

another flip-flop. She needed to get control of herself. It must be the Tuscan sun that was affecting her.

'What did you see?'

'Everything in the tourist guide. The Ponte Vecchio, the Uffizi, the church of Santa Maria Novella. I've walked until my feet ache.'

'What is this History of Art that you are studying?' He crossed his long legs in front of him and settled back against his seat.

'Oh, you kind of learn about the history of art.' She flushed again. Talk about stating the obvious. But this man was addling her brain and making her tongue-tied. 'I mean it's learning about artists—like Michelangelo, for example, how he became a sculptor, all the art he did and why that's considered important.'

There was a pause and Dante frowned. 'What do you do with this degree when you are finished studying?'

Good question and not one that she wanted to answer. People in her position weren't expected to do proper jobs. Modelling was okay, as long as it wasn't glamour, so was PR, as was fundraising. Even these were considered to be ways of passing the time until marriage and children came along. Her role was to run her father's house and carry out all the duties and responsibilities that went with her title.

She realised Dante was still waiting for an answer to his question.

'Actually, when I was a little girl I dreamt of becoming a teacher.'

'So, why didn't you?'

Why hadn't she? Because she'd always known that her life had been mapped out in an entirely different direction. One over which she had no control.

'It was just a childish dream. Nothing more.'

Brown eyes locked onto hers. 'It is good to dream, no?' He was studying her as if she puzzled him.

No, it wasn't good to dream. Not for her. It only made real life more difficult.

'We all have to live in the real world, don't we?' she replied lightly.

'Have you been out to the country?' Alice was relieved when he changed the subject.

She shook her head. She had been too absorbed sightseeing and exploring all the touristy attractions Florence had to offer to venture further afield.

'If you have not been in the countryside, then you have not seen Tuscany properly. Maybe I will show you.'

Alice wiped the palms of her hands on her trousers. He was only being polite. He would probably forget about her the moment he left her.

'You said you live in the mountains,' she asked. 'But you work in Florence?'

Again that expressive shrug of the shoulders. 'I work here, at this hospital, but my home is about forty-five kilometres that way, near where Sofia lives.' He gestured behind him. 'How long do you have left here in Tuscany?' he continued.

'Another week. I'll be sorry to leave.'

'You are staying in Florence?'

Alice nodded. 'A friend of my father's has a

home here. He's happy for me to use it while I'm visiting.'

'You are here on your own?' Dante seemed a little shocked.

'Yes, but I don't mind. In fact I kind of like it.'

Dante looked disbelieving.

'Would you like to meet me in the Piazza della Signoria tomorrow?' he asked. 'You can't leave without seeing the real Tuscany and I would like to show you more of my country.'

Alice shuffled uncomfortably in her seat. Part of her wanted to spend more time with him. Another part knew it was a crazy idea. What could she and this man possibly have in common?

'I'm not sure. I don't think it's a good idea.'

He looked at her with languid eyes. 'I think it is a very good idea.'

One thing she could say about him, he didn't give up easily.

'I was in London once for a month and a family there looked after me,' he said. 'I would like to show the same hospitality to our visitors. To you. And you helped Sofia when you didn't need to.

You could have walked away like everyone else, but you didn't.'

Alice flushed. Despite what she had just told herself, it was disappointing that he felt it was his duty to show her around.

Whatever his reasons, seeing him again was too risky. He was different from any man she had ever met and never before had a man made her pulse race the way Dante did. The last thing she was looking for was a holiday romance. She smiled. She was getting way ahead of herself. Someone like him was bound to have a girl-friend, although she'd already noticed he wasn't wearing a wedding ring.

The doors to the department opened and a distracted couple rushed in. Instinctively Alice knew these were Sofia's parents, not least be-cause the little girl was almost a carbon copy of her mother.

Dante jumped to his feet. 'Please meet me there at three o'clock tomorrow, I am working until two,' he told Alice as he went to intercept the distressed couple. After talking to them for a few moments, he led them towards the lift. Alice guessed he was taking them to see their little girl. Alice stared after his retreating back. The arrogance of the man! He hadn't even waited to hear her reply.

Alice was a nervous wreck by the time three o'clock the next day came. She had braided her hair, noticing that over the last week the sun had lightened it to almost the colour of corn which in turn emphasised the unusually light green colour of her eyes. She had dressed simply, in a crisp white blouse and light trousers. Apart from a slick of pale lipstick she didn't bother with any other make-up. For the umpteenth time she wondered if Dante would come. It was entirely possible he had forgotten all about her.

But he was waiting for her on the same steps that she'd been sitting on the previous day.

'*Ciao*, Alice,' he said, and kissed her on either cheek. 'I thought we could have a picnic down on the river then I will take you to see more of Florence. How does that sound?'

He took her to the river bank and they sat on the grass. He pointed to a woman rowing on the river. 'It is like I do. The boat I row is for a single person, but I know where I can get one for two. Maybe tomorrow I can take you?'

Alice's pulse skipped a beat. He was already planning their next date.

She looked down at the effort Dante had put into their picnic. There was a round of cheese, several types of cold meats, Tuscan bread and olives, as well as fresh salad leaves. This wasn't lunch, this was a feast.

'The olives and salad come from our smallholding and my mother bakes the bread herself. Of course, there is a *trattoria* not far from here. We could go there instead.'

Alice shook her head. She had had her fill of restaurants, fancy or otherwise. It was perfect here in the sun.

'*Bene*, we will eat then we will have time for me to show you something.'

The food Dante had brought was so delicious she found she had eaten more than her fair share.

'I'm sorry. I've eaten more than I should, but it was so delicious.'

'You must never apologise for enjoying food.' He leaned back on his elbows and regarded her through slitted eyes. 'Most women, they are too thin—as if they are starving. All the men I know prefer women who have some curves. Like Botticelli's *Venus*.' He grinned at her. 'Have you seen any statues in Florence where the women look like men? I don't think so.'

The look in his eyes was doing all sorts of weird things to her stomach. Hastily she took another forkful of salad and nearly choked.

Dante sat up, looking concerned.

'Are you okay?'

How attractive, Alice thought furiously. Spitting bits of lettuce leaf all over him. And right enough, to her mortification, Dante lifted his hand and very gently removed something from the corner of her mouth.

'That's better.' He was laughing at her and Alice was tempted to abandon her lunch and run back to the villa. It was the first time she had ever felt gauche and awkward. Until she'd come to Italy, she had used her expensive clothes and jewellery almost like an invisible cloak to hide her natural shyness.

He stood up. 'So you have seen the statue of David, the Uffizi and the church of Santa Maria Novella.' Alice was pleased that he'd remembered what she'd told him.

'Did you climb to the top of the Duomo and look down at the city?'

Alice shook her head. 'It was too hot to stand in the queue.'

He held out a hand to her. 'But you must see it. Come, I will take you if you like. It is a little climb but it is worth it. I have a cousin who works there. He will let us come to the front so we don't have to wait.'

'No, that's not fair. We should wait our turn like everybody else.'

Dante frowned. 'Here in Italy, we are not so polite. But if you don't want to go to the Duomo, there is another place just a short drive from here where you can see the city. The view is as good as that from the Duomo. When I run in the afternoons after work, I like to go past it and I always have to stop and look. I have my motorbike nearby. We could drive there now.'

Alice nodded and to her surprise he took her by the hand and yet somehow it felt natural. She felt a ripple of excitement as he led her through the narrow streets until they came to a number of motorbikes, haphazardly parked next to each other. It looked to Alice as if the owners had abandoned them there. When he'd mentioned a motorbike, Alice had assumed Dante meant a moped, like every other young Italian seemed to own. She baulked at the powerful-looking Kawasaki, eyeing it with trepidation. 'You won't go too fast?'

He laughed. 'Going fast is the fun of it. But don't worry, you'll be safe with me. I promise.'

She found herself on the back of his Kawasaki and soon he was weaving his way in and out of the traffic, gesticulating good-naturedly as cars tried to cut them up. More than once Alice thought they were going to crash and closed her eyes only to find that they had managed, at the last moment, to squeeze through a gap she hadn't even noticed. She wound her arms tightly around his waist and pressed her face into his back so she wouldn't have to look. He smelled faintly of olives and soap and she could feel the heat from his body through her clothes. Every part of her body was tingling where it touched him.

At first Alice kept her eyes closed. If she was going to die, she'd rather not see it coming, but after a little while she opened them again. She couldn't spend the whole day with her eyes closed. Then she relaxed. She had never felt so free in all her life.

Dante was right; the view from the top of the hill was breathtaking. Spread beneath her, a golden red in the dying sun, were the terracotta roofs of Florence. The city didn't look nearly as big and bewildering from up here.

They sat on a low wall as Dante pointed out the famous landmarks of the city—the Campanile, Santa Croce, the brick tower of the Palazzo Vecchio. His pride in his home city was evident.

They sat there talking, though later Alice couldn't remember about what. It didn't seem to matter to either of them. The sun dipped low in the sky and the lights of the city twinkled below them. A cool breeze teased her neck and she shivered, yet she didn't want this evening to end.

'Are you cold, *cara*?' Dante asked, putting an arm around her shoulders and pulling her towards him. Alice leant against him, her hand pressed against his chest. The air between them sizzled and sparked and she turned her face towards him, noting how his eyes seemed to glimmer in the dark. As Dante traced a finger down her cheek a delicious shiver ran down her spine. Using the tips of his fingers, he tilted her face upwards and studied her intently, before bringing his mouth down on hers.

The kiss was the sweetest and yet the most exciting Alice had ever known. When he pulled away, she could hardly breathe. She barely knew this man, yet she already knew something special was happening to her.

* * *

Later that night, after Dante had dropped Alice back outside her villa, he sped along the mountain road, weaving between cars and revelling in the feel of the wind on his face. As he concentrated on hugging the tight turns he thought about Alice. *Dio*, she was sexy with her long blonde hair and eyes the colour of the hills. She had curves that made a man want to run his hands across her body. And those lips, they tasted like honey and pears. He found her even more sexy because she had no idea what she could do to a man. She was shy and inexperienced and he wondered if she'd ever been with a man before. But it wasn't just the way she looked that set his blood on fire, in her heart she was different to the women he usually dated. The opposite of Natalia.

Thinking about Natalia still made him angry. They had grown up together and everyone had expected them to marry. But when he had decided to become a doctor, he and Natalia had argued. She'd wanted him to go into business with her father, telling Dante that that way they could have a good life. A rich life was what she'd meant. Of course he had refused. He was going to be a doctor—it was what he was meant to do. Natalia had stamped her foot and argued that she couldn't—wouldn't—wait until he was earning money. So she had left and married someone else. Now she was living the life she had always wanted. Since Natalia he had never let another woman close.

But he had been attracted to Alice instantly. He had asked her to meet him on an impulse, but to his surprise he'd found he enjoyed her company. He'd had many women since Natalia but they weren't like Alice. They cared more about what they were wearing, what they looked like, and that was fine. But soon it got boring. He liked a woman who could talk, who knew how to laugh, who loved the simple things in life. Like Alice. Already he knew she could never pretend to be something she wasn't.

He opened the throttle to pass a lorry that was lumbering up the mountain road and just managed to squeeze into the gap between it and an oncoming car. He laughed out loud. *Dio*, that was closer than he would have liked.

He had ten days to spend with Alice before she returned to the UK and he was going to make the most of them.

The next days were the most exciting of Alice's life. She met Dante every afternoon after he finished work at the hospital. He showed her a side of Italy, the real Italy, that she'd never seen before, and every day she fell harder for him. If he was puzzled that she always insisted that he drop her off at the high walls shielding the villa where she was staying, he never said anything. He waited until the gates opened in response to her pressing the buzzer before he sped away on his bike. Alice knew she should tell him who she really was, but she wanted the dream-like state she was in to go on for ever.

Saturday was his day off and that morning, her second last day in Italy, he picked her up from outside the villa on his motorbike. He held out a helmet and as he helped with the straps his fingers brushed her throat. Her skin literally sizzled where he'd touched her.

'Where are we going?' she asked.

His eyes seemed to glow as he looked down at her. 'I want you to see where I live. Will you come?'

Alice's heart thumped against her ribs. There was something in those dark eyes that told her that he wasn't asking her just because he wanted to show her where he lived.

Dry-mouthed, she could only nod.

Dante drove his bike as if he were pursued by a hundred devils, overtaking when there was the smallest of gaps.

Eventually, after the scariest but most exhilarating forty minutes of Alice's life, they drove down a dirt track before stopping next to an olive grove.

Alice eased herself off the motorbike hoping that her shaking legs would hold her. She just about managed to hobble a few steps before Dante pulled her into the crook of his arm. She leant into him, savouring the warmth of his body.

'This is where I grew up,' he said, gesturing towards the trees. 'Behind this is my mother's house and a little further is the building where I live. It used to be for the shepherds, but now it is my home.'

She turned in his arms, relaxing against his chest. Behind her, he wrapped his arms more tightly around her. In the cocoon of his arms she felt at peace. She had never felt so happy. And she had never felt so sad. Her time with Dante was drawing to an end too quickly. Through the thin material of his T-shirt she could feel his heart beating and knew hers was keeping time with his.

'Will you come with me to my house?' he asked. His voice vibrated through her and her heart kicked hard against her ribs. She knew what he was asking.

She turned in his arms until she was looking directly into his eyes.

'Yes,' she said.

'*Via*,' he said. He wasn't smiling any longer. His dark eyes were intense, almost black.

He took her hand and led her down a path
through the olive trees.

Once they were hidden from any passing cars,
he pulled her back into his arms. For one long
moment they looked into each other's eyes and
then he was kissing her. His mouth tasted of
tomatoes and sunshine. A pool of liquid lust
spread from her belly downwards and upwards
until every part of her body felt as if it was on
fire. If he carried on kissing her like this she
would surely spontaneously combust. Even as
he was kissing her she was smiling.

Dante pulled his head back while keeping her
body pressed close into his. She could feel every
inch of him along the length of her body.

'What is funny?' Although he half smiled, his
eyes were glittering.

'Nothing. Everything. I'm happy,' she said
simply.

'*Amore*, I have never met someone as honest as
you before. I like it,' Dante said, and then he was
kissing her again. Until she had met him, she had
never been kissed like that before. She had never

been held like this before. She had never felt like this before.

He pushed her gently against a tree and gathered her hands in his, pinning them above her head. She couldn't stop this. Not if her life depended on it.

His eyes raked across her body, lingering on her breasts. He kissed her throat at the point where her pulse was beating wildly. Still holding her wrists with one hand, he dropped his other hand to the buttons of her blouse. Alice could dimly hear the sounds of cars passing on the nearby road but as he slowly unbuttoned her blouse, all awareness of the outside world left her. '*Tesoro mio*,' he murmured, dropping kisses ever lower.

She arched her neck and raked her hands through his thick, dark hair. Each of his kisses was sending hot flames through her body. She almost couldn't bear it. She felt as if she was going to lose control. She had to stop this. He'd called her honest. She needed to tell him the truth.

But she couldn't call a halt. The only thing that mattered was the here and now.

Dante had pushed her blouse aside and was kissing her breasts. He circled her nipples with his tongue and ripples of pure, exquisite pleasure throbbed through her aching body.

Suddenly, to her dismay, he stopped. She moaned and tried to draw his head back down but Dante shook his head and slowly, reluctantly released her arms. His eyes were black with desire.

He buttoned up her blouse. Dazed, she could only watch.

'Not here,' he said hoarsely.

She knew what he was saying and she was powerless to resist. In a couple of days she would be home, back to being Lady Alice. Right now, all she wanted to do, all she ached for was to be back in his arms. She would tell him the truth. If whatever this thing was that was between them had a chance, she had to be as honest as he thought she was.

As they walked towards Dante's house, Alice thought her heart would break. Two more nights, then she'd be returning to her life in London. The thought of leaving was tearing her in two.

The air was rich with the scent of olives as he led her by the hand through the orchard. Within a few minutes they arrived at a small whitewashed building with an ochre roof standing on its own in a little oasis of green.

Still holding her by the hand, Dante opened the door and pulled her inside. Alice only had a fleeting glimpse of a double bed before Dante was kissing her again.

Later, much later she lay with her head on his chest. He stroked her hair and murmured to her in Italian.

She traced the scar on his shoulder with the tip of her finger.

'How did this happen?' she asked.

'An accident with my motorbike. Two years ago. A lorry came round on the wrong side of the road. I had to go into a ditch to miss it.'

'You could have been killed!' Alice said, alarmed.

'But I wasn't. I was hurt. A few days in hospital. It wasn't so bad. My girlfriend at that time wasn't happy.'

'Have there been lots of women?' she asked. She could have bitten her tongue the moment the words were out. Of course there had been lots of women. She could tell that from the way Dante had made love to her. As if she was precious, but also with passion and an uncanny sense of what she needed and when.

His hands paused in her hair.

'A few. But they were not important—' He broke off. 'I've never met anyone quite like you.'

The warm glow of happiness she'd experienced since they'd made love deepened. But under the glow she felt a shiver of unease. What would he think of her when he found out she hadn't been honest with him? She wasn't who he thought she was. Reluctant to spoil the mood, Alice raised herself on her elbow and looked down at him. 'Why did you decide to become a doctor?' she asked.

He sat up and pulled her head against his chest

where she could hear the strong beat of his heart. One of his hands was in her hair, the other softly caressing her neck. Everywhere he touched her sent stabs of desire coursing through her body. She hadn't known that a simple touch on her skin could drive her wild with longing.

When his answer came his voice was deeper than ever.

'A few years ago, I had a friend. A girl, Rosa. We had played with each other since we were children.' His hands paused on her skin and he took a deep breath.

'Her house was next to mine. We were always together. At school. After school. While we were growing up. Soon she was no longer a little girl but a beautiful woman.'

A stab of jealousy so strong it took her breath away ripped through Alice.

'Did you love her?' she asked, trying to keep her voice casual.

Dante laughed. '*Sì*, I loved her, but we were never lovers. She was like a sister to me.' His voice grew sombre again. 'I didn't know what I wanted to do with my life, but she always knew what she wanted to do. To be a nurse.' He paused and Alice knew he was remembering. 'I stayed on the farm and she went to university. The first holiday she came back, it was as if we had never been parted. She was so excited with what she was learning. She was lit up inside. But after a few days she got sick.'

Dante's voice was like sandpaper. Alice held her breath and waited for him to go on.

'Everyone thought it was flu. No one was worried. Her mother phoned the doctor. He told her it wasn't a problem, to give Rosa painkillers for the headache and fever. By the time she came out in a rash, it was too late.'

'Meningitis?' Alice whispered.

'*Sì.* It was before the time they vaccinated against it. We called the ambulance. I knew it would take too long. I didn't want to wait. We were losing her.'

He paused again and swallowed. 'We put her in the car and I drove as fast as I could. But it was too late. By the time we got to the hospital, she was unconscious. I would have given my life for her, but I wasn't able to do one thing to save her. It is why I became a doctor. I will never let anyone die because I didn't know how to help them.'

'I'm so sorry, Dante.'

'You are like her in many ways. Kind and honest.'

Another spasm of guilt ran up Alice's spine. She had to tell him.

'You are different from other women.' There was a note of bitterness in his voice that puzzled Alice. 'You don't care about material things. Clothes. Money. What other people think of you.'

Alice's heart felt as if it were slowly being encased in ice. When she told him the truth about herself, he would see that she wasn't the woman he thought she was. She couldn't bear that. Was there any point in telling him? In two days she would be gone.

Propping herself on her elbow, she gazed down at his beautiful face. He was smiling.

'You don't really know me, Dante,' she said softly.

'I know enough. But there is more to learn, I think.' The look in his eyes as they travelled across her body set nerve endings she'd never even known she had on fire. He pushed her back down on the bed and nibbled her ear. 'You could stay in Florence longer,' he murmured. 'Don't you have more time before you have to go back to university?'

Alice felt her heart plummet down to her toes. Was that all he wanted from her? Just another few days of a holiday romance—and then what?

Almost as if reading her mind, Dante pushed himself up on his powerful arms and gazed down at her. 'Or maybe longer than that. You could stay with me,' he said softly.

It was as if someone had dropped ice cubes down the back of her neck. He couldn't know how impossible it was for her to do what he was asking. When he found out who she truly was, he would feel differently about her and she couldn't bear that. Already she knew she was falling in love with him and the longer she stayed the harder she would fall. The thought terrified her. She had to leave before she got in any deeper. No matter how much she wanted to stay with him—more than anything she had ever wanted—there could never be a future for them. Her father needed her. She had her life and shallow though it was, it was the only life she knew.

Not that Dante was suggesting anything more than a few more days together.

She ran her fingertips across his chest down towards the silky hair of his abdomen. He drew a sharp breath as she let her hands travel lower. With him she felt no shyness, only a sense of wonder at the power her touch had over him.

In response he brushed his hand along the inside of her thigh and her bones turned to mush. '*Amore mio*,' he growled, 'I can't think when you do that.' His hands travelled higher up her thigh and he groaned. 'That's enough talking for now. We'll talk more tomorrow.'

But Alice already knew there would be no tomorrow for them. She knew with heart-breaking certainty that they only had a few hours. She would have to make the most of every second.

CHAPTER ONE

ALICE studied herself in the full-length mirror. Her dress, a shimmer of silver, clung to her body before falling in a little train at the back. These days she no longer had to worry about revealing curves that suggested an over-enthusiastic fondness for food. Not eating tended to do that.

As soon as she'd come back to London she'd broken off with Peter, much to her father's disappointment. Peter was everything he'd hoped for in a son-in-law. But he wasn't Dante. Alice knew she could never marry anyone who didn't make her feel the way Dante had, even if that meant being single for the rest of her life.

She pursed her lips as she applied deep red lipstick, trying to dispel the empty feeling that lurked somewhere deep inside. Okay, so this wasn't how she'd envisaged her life to turn out, but she was happy, maybe not happy in that scary, intense way she had felt in Italy—she doubted she'd ever feel like that again—but she was content, wasn't she? At least with her new, more active role with the charity she was doing some good. This fundraiser would bring in thousands of pounds for the camps for the displaced in Africa. And if she felt empty inside, as if someone had taken a giant ice-cream scoop and hollowed her out, didn't lots of people feel that way? She should count her blessings, as people always said. Underneath the empty feeling was one of excitement. She was going to Africa with the charity. Maybe out there she would find the Alice she had been in Italy. Maybe, at last, she'd feel as if her life had some meaning.

She finished her make-up and tucked a stray lock of hair behind her ear. Bless Susan, she knew exactly how do her hair so that it would stay firmly in place for the whole evening.

Alice glanced at her watch. Almost time to go.

She sighed at her image in the mirror. A pale face with dark shadows stared back at her. Had it really been a year since she had said goodbye to Dante? Tonight the guest speaker, who was doing a presentation on behalf of the charity for which this evening was being held, was a Dr Salvatore, who was coming from the same hospital where Dante had worked. When she'd seen his name on the programme, she'd contemplated slipping in a casual question to Dr Salvatore about Dante. He was bound to know him.

She knew she was torturing herself, especially if Dante turned out to be engaged or, worse still, married, but she was desperate to hear about him, even if it was only someone saying his name. When she'd left Italy without saying goodbye, she'd told herself it was for the best. So why did her heart still ache for him?

But she mustn't think of Dante. Not tonight. Even though barely a day went past when she didn't think of his deep brown eyes. And his smile. All that was safely in the past. She was living the life she was meant to live. Italy had been a dream. A wonderful dream. She had to look to the future.

Downstairs, the ballroom was thronging with guests. All willing to pay thousands of pounds for a seat at the dinner table, knowing that the money would be put to good use. Alice could see the top of her father's head as he spoke animatedly to someone. Knowing him, it would be another business deal. Dad wasn't one to waste an opportunity. Not when the heads of businesses from across the world were in this room.

The room sparkled from the hundreds of lights from the oversized chandeliers. The tables were set with the finest crystal money could buy and at each table setting there was a little Swarovski souvenir for the guests to take home. The heavy scent of lilies drifted from tall crystal vases. In the corner a string quartet was playing softly. At the end of the evening there would be a surprise for the guests as her father had flown in a famous opera singer to round off the evening. Alice couldn't help but wonder if some of the money her father had lavished on this event could have been better spent. Given to the charity, for example. But when she'd raised the issue with him, he'd assured her that the money the evening would bring in would far outstrip the money he had lavished on this dinner. Not least as he had already personally pledged a significant sum.

The room was already packed. Diamonds flashed from throats and wrists as women in elegant evening gowns lifted glasses to their lips. The men were in dinner jackets and bow-ties, and the murmur of low voices and the occasional rumble of laughter filtered above the sound of the music.

As she weaved her way through the crowd towards her father, people parted to let her past. She paused to accept a glass of champagne from a passing waiter.

Suddenly there was a hush and all eyes swivelled towards the door. A tall, dark-haired man was standing by the entrance. He was wearing a leather jacket over a pale mauve shirt and black trousers. But it wasn't his casual dress that caused everyone to follow his process across the room, it was his presence. A sort of natural elegance coupled with an arrogance—a way of holding his head, a half-smile on his lips as he gazed around the room with slitted, amused eyes.

Alice had stopped with her glass midway to her lips. His hair was shorter, much shorter, and there were creases near his eyes and mouth that hadn't been there before, but there was no doubt. It was Dante and he was walking towards her father.

Her legs almost buckled. She hadn't seen him in twelve months but every part of her came alive as if a bolt of lightning had coursed through her body. What was he doing here? Where was Dr Salvatore?

She glanced around, thinking that she would escape to the ladies to give her time to get her trembling hands under control, but just then her father called her name and gestured to her to come over to him. If she fled now, she would look like an idiot. Taking a deep breath, she squared her shoulders and fixed a smile on her face. Hadn't she taught herself to do that whenever she found herself in a difficult situation? And this one was off the Richter scale as far as difficult situations went.

'Alice! My dear. I'd like you to meet Dr Dante Corsi. One of the directors of People in Need. Dr Corsi, my daughter, Lady Alice.'

As Alice looked into deep brown eyes the room began to spin. In a single second she was transported back to Florence, to his bed in his cottage. All the moments she had so miserly treasured and so desperately tried to forget.

Once more, years of training in how to handle difficult social situations came to Alice's rescue.

She saw the shock of recognition in Dante's eyes then quickly the shutters came down.

'Dr Corsi and I have already met.' She proffered her face for a kiss, only too aware of the familiar scent of his aftershave as he bent his head and kissed her on either cheek.

'Oh!' Her father looked puzzled for a moment then his brow cleared. 'In Italy, of course. But how?'

'Your daughter was trying her hand as an artist. There was an accident. She helped me care for the victims. It was a long time ago.' Dante lowered his voice. 'How have you been?' His voice was matter-of-fact, his face expressionless, but his eyes were saying all sorts of things. Stuff she didn't want to hear. Like who the hell are you? Why did you leave without saying goodbye?

Alice's father narrowed his eyes. She could almost see his sharp, analytical brain whirling.

'Dr Corsi is here to do a presentation on behalf of one of the charities we are raising money for tonight,' he told Alice.

'You raise money for the charity?' Alice tried hard to keep her voice even. But it was difficult with her heart hammering away like a steam train. 'I thought you were still working as a paediatrician in Florence.'

She realised her mistake as soon as the words were out of her mouth. Now he'd know that she'd been keeping track on his career. But she hadn't known about his work with the charity. And she certainly hadn't known he'd be here. If she had, she would have found some excuse not to come.

Dante's eyes were as dark as the night outside. 'What about you? Did you finish your degree? How have you been?' He sounded almost bored.

'Yes, I finished my degree,' she said softly. 'At the moment, I raise funds for the charity my father sponsors.' She knew she sounded defensive.

Alice's father was looking from one to another, puzzlement still written all over his face. Then someone waved, trying to catch his attention.

'Would you excuse me for a moment?' her father said. 'There's someone I need to speak to. I'll be back shortly.'

Don't go, Daddy, Alice wanted to shout. *Don't leave me alone with this man.* But of course she couldn't say anything. She smiled faintly.

'So, *Lady* Alice, 'Dante drawled, his voice heavy with sarcasm, 'I see now why you left in such a hurry.' His eyes were cold.

'Not here, Dante, not now,' she muttered. She could not have this conversation with everyone watching them with curious eyes.

He grabbed her by the elbow and steered her towards the open French windows. She tried to pull her arm away but his grip was too strong.

She couldn't risk making a scene so she let him propel her outside onto the roof terrace.

Although seating had been set out on the terrace, most people were still inside. A fountain sprayed water into the air and the lights of London glittered as far as the eye could see.

At least the early summer breeze cooled her burning cheeks. Dante spun her towards him.

'So. Now I've found you, are you going to tell me why you never told me who you really were?'

Her mouth was dry and her heart was hammering so hard she thought she was going to pass out. How could she explain? In retrospect it seemed ridiculous that she hadn't told him, but what had been the point? There had never been any question of she and Dante having a future together. In the cold light of the day after they'd made love Alice had run, knowing that she was already more than a little in love with him and knowing that a long-term future together was impossible.

'You l-looked for m-me?' she stuttered.

'I waited for you at the piazza and when you

didn't turn up I thought something had happened to you.' A small muscle twitched in his cheek. '*Dio*, I thought you'd had an accident—that you might be lying in a hospital wondering why I didn't come to you. I went to the villa but it was locked up, apart from the housekeeper. She told me you had left and that, no, she couldn't give me your address. You didn't even have the courage to tell me you were going. Then I got the letter you left for me at the hospital.' He smiled but there was no humour in his eyes. 'At least I knew you were not hurt.'

'I…' Alice took a deep breath. 'You're right. I should have told you I was leaving. I'm sorry.'

Dante jammed his hands into his pockets as if to prevent himself from reaching out and shaking her. He lifted an eyebrow. 'Sorry?' This time his smile was positively cat-like. He shrugged. 'It does not matter. I made a mistake. I thought you were different. I was wrong.'

Anger rose up like a tidal wave. Okay, so she should have told him she was leaving, but he had never pretended she was anything more to him than a holiday romance.

'You have no right to judge me, Dante. As you pointed out, you don't know the first thing about my life here.'

'Because you chose not to tell me.' There was no mistaking the contempt in his eyes. 'You did not have to lie.'

'I didn't lie,' she said hotly. When he raised an eyebrow she added hastily, 'I just didn't tell you the truth.' It sounded weak even to her own ears.

'It is the same thing,' he said quietly. 'You should have trusted me. Instead you chose to act out a little...' he struggled to find the right word '...play.'

'Here you are.' Peter's voice cut through the tension that lay between them like a thick layer of fog. 'I've been looking for you everywhere.' Although they were no longer engaged, they were still friendly.

Dante looked at Peter and his eyes turned black.

'Peter, this is Dr Corsi, who is here on behalf of the charity.'

'I'm pleased to meet you, Dr Corsi,' Peter said. 'I understand that the staff is ready to help you set up for your presentation.'

'Pronto.' Dante dipped his head at Peter and swung on his heel, leaving Alice alone with Peter.

'What is it? You're pale. Almost as if you've seen a ghost. Are you feeling all right?'

No, she was not feeling all right. And, yes, she had just seen a ghost.

Alice took a deep breath and squared her shoulders. Somehow she would have to get through this evening.

'I'm fine. It was hot in there and I was feeling a little faint so Dr Corsi suggested getting some fresh air. I feel much better now. Shall we take our seats?'

Alice didn't know how she got through dinner. Although the food had been cooked by a famous London chef especially for the occasion, every bite tasted like sawdust and Alice found it difficult to swallow. Now and then, when she looked up from her plate, she would find Dante's eyes on her. She forced herself to concentrate on her dinner companions, but crazy thoughts were running through her head. Dante had looked for her. Was that why he was here instead of Dr Salvatore? Had he seen her name and recognised it and decided to come here to berate her? No, she couldn't believe it. Dante wasn't small minded.

After dinner was cleared away, Dante rose to his feet and took his place on a raised platform at the front of the room.

Dante's presentation tugged at the heartstrings. He showed a film of the camp he represented. There were pictures of women with children in their laps and arms. The camera focussed on one in particular. The child was tiny, her dark brown eyes enormous as she looked into the camera.

'How old do you think this child is?' Dante asked the audience. 'Two years? Three?' He paused as the room stirred. 'I can tell you that this little girl is actually seven years old.'

There was an audible gasp from the people sitting around the table. If they had come for an evening of socialising and entertainment, they had just been reminded of the real reason they were there.

'There has been another drought this year and many villagers have left their homes in search of food and medicine. They walk for days to reach the camps. And these are the lucky ones—if they make it to the camp, that is. Two-thirds of the population live in villages where there is no help from the international community.'

The camera panned across the camp, stopping for a moment on the faces of the people huddled in a group. The faces were gaunt, the expressions hopeless. 'This particular camp already has one hundred and thirty thousand refugees and is one of the largest on earth. Our camp is a fraction of the size but it will get bigger and as it does we will need more of everything, especially more wells for clean water, and medical supplies.'

Dante spoke passionately, not just for the need for funding for the camps but for the need for trained volunteers. Still in shock, Alice couldn't believe that he was there. It didn't even seem to be the same man she had spent time with a year ago. This was a side to Dante that she hadn't seen before. He was as different from the fun-loving man she had known in Italy as it was possible to be. A part of her noted that while his English had always been good, it was better now. Although still heavily accented, it was perfect.

As she looked at the images flashing across the large screen, Alice felt something shift inside and a tingle of excitement ran up her spine. Soon she'd be there. Not at this camp, but one like it. Could she help make a difference? And would it help fill this empty space inside her?

After the talk, which was greeted with enthusiastic applause, a professional auctioneer took Dante's place and everyone started competing for weeks on private islands and sole charters of luxurious yachts. Soon the bidding had risen to tens of thousands of pounds. Alice knew it was Dante's presentation that had stirred the people in the room into making such generous bids.

The band struck up again and couples took to the dance floor. Alice found herself standing next to her father and Dante.

'Dr Corsi was just telling me the name of the camp that he's going out to in a couple of weeks. It's the same one you're going to, darling. So you'll be there at the same time.'

Dante was going to the same place? Her knees turned to rubber.

'You are going too?' Dante questioned, drawing his eyebrows together in a frown. 'I didn't know.'

'Alice was a late addition,' her father explained. 'Unfortunately she missed the training weekend through other commitments, but the agency assured me they were still happy to have her.'

Alice flushed. The charity wouldn't have dared refuse the daughter of their biggest benefactor. She knew how it must sound to Dante's ears. It all sounded so casual. As if she was playing at being a volunteer.

'The camps require the volunteers to be fit and used to living in very basic conditions as well having a level head. The work doesn't suit everyone.' Dante looked directly into her eyes. 'They want someone committed.'

'I am committed,' Alice protested. 'I organise

at least one charity dinner or lunch every month.' God, that hadn't come out the way she'd intended. If anything, it made her seem even more dizzy.

Her father laughed. 'I have tried to tell her, Dr Corsi, that she'd be better off staying here and helping to raise funds, but my daughter can be stubborn when she makes her mind up about something.' He turned to Alice. 'Good grief, child, you can't even cook, let alone cope with the conditions Dr Corsi has been showing us. Besides, you're scared of insects, remember?'

The smile her father shared with Dante infuriated her. Who did Dad think he was to tell her what she could and couldn't do? But, then, isn't that what's been happening all your life? a small voice whispered back. Living your life to please others? Isn't that why you ran away from Dante in the first place?

'I'm sorry, Lord Granville,' Dante said, 'but we can't take passengers. Everyone at the camp has to do what they can to help.' He shook his head at Alice. '*Lacia fare*, don't worry, I'm sure the charity will release you from your obligation and find someone suitable.'

What a cheek. If Dante thought he was going to stop her going, he had another think coming. 'You have someone suitable. And she's standing here in front of you,' Alice said firmly. There was no way she was going to be fobbed off. She went to the gym so she was fit, and she had been camping. Okay, so it had been a five-star camping place, but that had to count for something and she didn't eat much. Not these days. And, most importantly, she was good at organising. Everyone wanted to come to her functions.

Her father shook his head and, spotting someone across the room, excused himself. Clearly he had no doubt that this was a passing whim and hoped that either Alice would change her mind or that Dante would refuse to take her.

'So you want to come to Africa?' Dante's voice was soft, but his eyes drilled into hers. 'Is it to make yourself feel better?' His hand swept across the room and up to the chandeliers. 'One of these lights would pay for a doctor for a year.'

He reached for her wrist where her favourite diamond bracelet sparkled with a thousand lights. 'And this? Who knows what this would pay for?'

Alice snatched her hand away. 'You have no right to judge me, Dante.'

'No, I don't. It is not as if you and I are anything to each other.' His eyes softened. 'Where is the woman I knew in Italy? Who is this woman who looks beautiful but cold, as if she has forgotten she has a heart?'

How dare he? He knew nothing about the woman she was now. She had changed. Italy and Dante had changed her. Gone was the woman who felt she had to live her life by pleasing others. Whilst she still had to attend parties and clubs, be seen at the right lunches and fashion shows, now it was for worthwhile causes. The second thing she'd done after breaking up with Peter had been telling her father she wanted to be more involved in the actual running of their charities. At first he'd given in, almost as if he was only humouring her. But she'd worked hard to prove to herself—and she had succeeded.

'I want to go,' she said. 'If you don't agree to take me, I'll set up my own group and go anyway. You may not be aware of this, but I have influence about the way money from the charity is directed.' It was a low blow and she knew it.

Dante narrowed his eyes and, despite the coldness she saw there, her heart dropped like a broken lift. Her brain was sending wild messages about staying away from him that she was refusing to acknowledge. Remember the man standing in front of you has been haunting your dreams for the last year. Remember how you felt when you were with him. Are you mad even to contemplate spending more time in his company?

'You will use your position and power to make me take you?' The contempt in his eyes was painful.

'If I have to.'

Once again that calculating look came back into his eyes.

'I'll tell you what, *cara*. I have to go back to Italy, to my home in the mountains. I will be there for a week before I have to leave for Africa.

If you can come to Italy in the next few days, I will take you hiking. If you can get up the mountain carrying your own rucksack and if you can camp at the top, I will think about taking you. All the other volunteers who go to camps in Africa have to do a similar challenge to make sure they are able to cope, so I think it is fair that you have to do it too. No?'

The look in his eyes told Alice he had no doubt she would fail at the task. Well, Dante didn't know her as well as he thought.

She held out her hand. 'It's a deal,' she said.

Back in his hotel room, Dante couldn't get Alice out of his head. When he'd seen her across the room, before she had seen him, he'd almost been unable to believe it was her. She looked so different, so calm and assured, like one of the women in glossy magazines. When he'd got closer, only then had he been sure that she was Alice. Despite the fancy hair and dress, he would never forget the vulnerable mouth that begged to be kissed or her strangely coloured green eyes, although the sadness he saw behind the shock had shaken him. She wasn't the woman he had thought she was, that much he knew. Who *was* the woman he'd known in Italy? The one with the shining eyes and the ready smile? The woman who had almost made him believe again? After Natalia he had promised himself he would never let another woman get under his skin. And he hadn't. He had dated women, many women, but none of them had got as close to thawing his heart as Alice. Never would he open his heart to any woman again. Least of all this one.

Still fully clothed, he lay down on the bed, knowing he wouldn't sleep.

As for coming to Africa. What was that about? Was this another part she wanted to play?

She could come to Italy. That would make her see that the idea of her in Africa was ridiculous. He felt a surge of amusement. Alice would never manage the trek up the mountain, not least because he would make sure it was tough. Not too difficult so that she could claim he had made it impossible, but hard enough. She'd probably give up before they'd even reached the halfway point, then she would see for herself that coming to Africa was out of the question. She'd be out of his life for good and he wouldn't have jeopardised the funding for the camp.

He placed his hands behind his head. All in all he had managed everything to his satisfaction. And if green eyes the colour of the Tuscan hills in spring lingered in his mind, that was only to be expected. She was still the most beautiful woman he knew, even if she wasn't to be trusted.

CHAPTER TWO

'*Dio*, what is that you are wearing?'

Alice followed Dante's gaze down to her shiny new walking boots.

'My boots. Why? What's wrong with them? The shop assistant assured me they were the best boots money could buy. He even said I could climb Everest with them.'

Alice had spent the few days shopping for the right gear. Apart from the boots she had bought a rucksack, waterproof trousers, a new windbreaker, thick socks, a travel hairdryer and a pair of pyjamas. She considered herself pretty much prepared for anything.

'But they are new? You haven't worn them before?'

'Of course I have,' Alice protested. She had worn them in her flat for at least a couple of hours before deciding that they didn't quite go with her skirt.

'You cannot wear new boots for a climb. You will get blisters.' Dante looked irritated and exasperated. He shook his head.

'They'll be fine,' Alice insisted. Why was he making such a fuss about everything?

When Dante had picked her up from the airport the night before, he'd taken an astonished look at her luggage.

'Are these bags all yours?' he'd asked.

She followed his gaze. She had only brought the essentials. It wasn't her fault that they had filled three suitcases. After all, she wanted to be prepared for any eventuality.

Now he was giving her rucksack the same incredulous look.

'And what is it you have in there?'

'Just the necessities. You know, make-up, clothes, something to eat—that sort of thing.' She was quite pleased with how strict she'd been with herself.

He tested the weight of her bag with his hand.

'Take half of it out. All you need is a toothbrush and towel and a change of clothes.'

Alice felt her cheeks burning. Who was he to tell her what to do?

'Isn't there someone coming with us who can carry it?' she asked, looking around. Weren't there always porters on these kinds of trips?

'Do you see anyone else? No, *cara*. It is just you and me.'

She knew her face was getting redder. Reluctantly she removed half of her stuff and ran back inside to leave it with the rest of her belongings. Damn the man, he was deliberately making everything more difficult for her than it needed to be.

After he'd picked her up at the airport, Dante had driven her to her accommodation for the night. He'd hardly said a word during the journey, except to give her the details of their trip. And that was just as well. What could she say? Sorry I ran out on you? Sorry I left without a word?

They'd pulled up outside a nondescript building on the outskirts of Florence in the middle of the night, and Alice had been worried. Where were the bright lights of the hotel? She had been dying for a bath to wash the four-hour delay at Heathrow from her hair.

There hadn't been a hotel. Dante had taken her to a hostel. Seeing her look of surprise, he had turned to her.

'The charity funds overnight accommodation. We like to keep the costs down. Besides, it is more, how do you say, luxurious than anything you'll be sleeping in in Africa.' He shrugged his shoulders and his eyes had gleamed in the semi-darkness. 'But if you want to change your mind, there is still time. No hard feelings. I could still take you to a hotel and leave you there.' Was that hope or satisfaction in his voice? It was obvious he was keen to dump her at the very first opportunity.

'This will be fine.' What kind of wimp did he think she was if he thought that she'd be put off that easily? However, she couldn't help feeling bereft when he left her on the door step and sped away.

She had to share a dormitory with bunk beds—bunk beds!—with five other women but at least they were welcoming and friendly. The bathroom, if you could call it that, was a single shower at the end of a long corridor. There wasn't even a curtain to protect her privacy. And one of her roommates snored. Alice hardly slept a wink. Then, to top it all, there was no breakfast. At least, not one that was served. Everyone had brought their own. Thankfully one of the girls who had shared her room turned out to be an angel in disguise and happily shared her coffee and bread with Alice. If it hadn't been for her, Alice would be in a worse temper.

So this morning she was in no mood for Dante and his surly attitude. What was he trying to prove? Was he thinking that he'd put her off even before she'd taken one step up the mountain? Well, he was badly mistaken.

When she went back outside he was pacing up and down, looking at his watch.

'We'd better get going. We have a long walk in front of us.'

Alice bit back a groan when she felt the weight of her rucksack. Even without all the items she'd taken out it still weighed a ton. Thank God he had made her remove half of what she'd been planning to take. She was starting to wish she'd never volunteered for the whole crazy venture.

An hour later Alice's legs were killing her, and as for her back! She felt as if she'd been run over by a steamroller then it had reversed and driven over her again. Her hair was plastered to her scalp and she was certain that her face was as red as the waterproof she was wearing.

Not that the thing seemed to be keeping her from getting soaked. Ever since they had started the climb at six that morning the rain had been coming down in sheets. The last time Alice had been awake so early, she had been coming home from a party.

Two hours later she felt as if she was carrying a truck and was on the verge of tears. What had possessed her? What was she trying to prove? That she was someone he could admire? To see something else in his eyes that wasn't derision?

If getting up this mountain proved to him she was capable of coping with anything Africa had to offer, then she would do it. Even if it took everything she had.

She was here now and she was damned if she was going to beg Dante to take her back to the airport.

She blinked the rain out of her eyes and eyed his broad back balefully. He was carrying his backpack as well as a tent and both their sleeping bags plus all the supplies they needed for their overnight journey, as if it all weighed nothing.

He had changed. How and why Alice had no idea, but the mischievous Dante that she had known had metamorphosed into a silent, grim man who seemed not to know the meaning of small talk.

Tears pricked the back of her throat. Whether it was because of her feet, which were blistered just as Dante had predicted, or whether it was because she seemed to have made such an almighty mess of everything, or whether it was because she hated it that Dante seemed to despise her, she didn't know. All she wanted was for him to smile at her.

He turned around and glared at her.

'We need to make better time,' he said, 'if we want to set up camp before it gets dark.' Then his expression softened and he looked concerned. 'You are limping. Do your feet hurt? *Dio*, why didn't you tell me?'

It was on the tip of her tongue to say that, no, her feet were perfectly all right in her lovely new boots, but she knew that would be childish and irresponsible. If she didn't deal with her feet right now, she'd be in real trouble soon.

She nodded. 'You were right about the boots,' she conceded. 'It feels as if I have a blister the size of a football on one of my heels. I don't suppose you brought a first-aid kit?'

Dante's mouth twitched.

'Come. Let me see.'

He swung his rucksack off his shoulders and nodded at a rock. 'Sit there.'

Feeling sorry for herself, Alice perched on the rock. At least it was giving her aching body a chance to rest. Before she could stop him, Dante knelt at her feet and lifted a booted foot into his lap.

'Is it this one?'

Alice nodded.

He undid the lace of her boot and peeled off her sock. His fingertips on her overheated skin felt deliciously cool. No. She was going to ignore those little goose-bumps running up her leg right to her scalp.

'It looks sore,' he said. He looked at her with something like surprise and, could it be, respect. 'How long have you been walking like this? You should have told me earlier.'

He dug around in his rucksack until he found the first-aid kit. Efficiently he peeled away the protective backing of a special plaster for blisters and attached it to Alice's heel.

'We can go back,' he said softly. 'You don't have to do this.'

'Yes, I do,' Alice replied. 'Come on, let's get going.'

It was a little easier with the plaster, but nevertheless Alice had to concentrate on putting one leg in front of the other. The gym had never been like this. The gym was air-conditioned and she could stop and take a break anytime she liked. Neither had her personal trainer Simon been as ruthless or as quiet as the man whose back she was following. Simon had let her stop for rests whenever she'd wanted.

At last Dante called a halt. They found a rock on the hillside and Alice took her first proper look around. It was beautiful. As far as the eye could see, lush green hills stretched to the horizon. Far below she could make out the lines of vineyards and to the left of them an olive grove. In the distance a dog barked. Apart from that, it was perfectly still.

Dante pointed to a forest to their right.

'Do you see those trees there?' he asked.

Alice nodded.

'That is a chestnut forest. That is how my grandfather used to make a living. When we were young we used to go up with my father to help him.' Dante looked sombre. 'It was a good life for us children, running free for the whole summer when we weren't helping on the land, but for my grandfather and father it wasn't an easy life.'

Alice waited for him to go. She suspected that what he was telling her was important to him.

'My grandparents were not rich. Not at all. Sometimes all they had to eat for weeks was chestnuts. My father didn't even always have shoes. His parents couldn't afford to let him stay at school because they needed him to help on the smallholding. But in time he had to leave. He had an elder brother who was married with a family and the little farm could not support them all. So he came to Florence and learned to be a shoemaker. He probably made shoes for people like you and your family. Sometimes the people who bought the shoes would spend more on one pair than my father would make in a month or even two months.'

'I'm sorry,' Alice said simply. She didn't know what he expected her to say. It was hardly her fault that she had been brought up in extreme wealth. On the other hand, how often had she thought about what it was like for those who didn't have money? Not often enough was the simple truth.

'You don't have to be sorry,' Dante said. 'I'm not telling you this because I want to make you feel bad. I had a happy childhood, happier than yours maybe?'

Alice swallowed hard. 'My childhood was fine,' she said. The last thing she wanted was him to probe. It was hard enough keeping it all together as it was.

He looked at her intently before continuing. 'Sometimes the three of us would go into the forest and shoot a wild boar. We would take it home for my grandmother to make *cinghiale prosciutto*. Those were good times.'

'There are wild boars in these mountains?' Alice looked around her, half expecting one to come crashing towards them. 'Aren't they dangerous?'

'They can be if you corner them. We get wolves too. Don't worry, they are more frightened of us than we are of them.'

Alice wasn't totally reassured, but she wasn't going to give him any more reasons to ridicule her.

'This place, the refugee camp, what's it like?' Alice thought it better to keep the conversation on neutral ground.

Dante passed her a bottle of water and Alice drank thirstily. Champagne had never tasted so good.

'It is in the north of Africa. It is very poor. Many people come there from all over the continent, sometimes walking for weeks. They think from there they can get on a boat and go to other countries. But there are no boats and even if they do find the money to pay someone to take them, the countries turn most of them back. Then they are in a worse position than ever before.' He shrugged his shoulders in the familiar gesture she knew so well.

'The people there are proud, but they need help. Malaria still kills too many of the children. And bad water. This camp we are going to is one of the newer ones. My colleagues have been there for a year now, so much has been done, but there is always more to do. When I go, it lets the doctor who is there for the whole time take a break for a few weeks.'

'How often do you go? What made you? What about your job at the hospital?'

Dante looked into the distance.

'When I met you I was finishing my training as a paediatrician. You remember?'

How could she forget? Every detail of that time was burnt into her memory.

'Money was short so I worked part-time with the Territorial Army to help put me through medical school.' He smiled and for a second Alice saw the Dante she had known. Almost immediately the mask came back down. 'After I finished my training I found I wanted to do more than just work as a doctor at the hospital. I was making money and that was good but I wanted to do more.

'I had a friend in the hospital, one of the other doctors, he told me about the organisation and the work they were doing. He said they are always looking for relief doctors, so every year I take four weeks of my vacation and go there. It helps that I was a doctor with the Territorial Army. The conditions can be tough.' He slid a glance at her. 'Very tough.'

It couldn't be any tougher than what she was having to go through right now.

'And you?' he continued after a moment. 'What happened to you?' he asked. 'Why didn't you tell me the truth about your life?'

Alice took a deep breath. 'Look, Dante, I should have been more honest with you about who I really was. I was wrong and I'm sorry. But you've had a glimpse of the life I lead and when I met you, I just wanted to be Alice.' How could she explain how much she had needed to be anonymous back then? She had never meant to deceive Dante, but who she was back home in England hadn't seemed important at first and then, when they had made love and she'd known she was going to leave, she hadn't been able to bear him to know she had been less than honest with him. 'I shouldn't have just have left, but it was impossible for me to stay. The time we had together in Italy was a dream. A lovely dream, but we all have to grow up some time.' As she said the words, she remembered their conversation the day they'd met. Hadn't he said that everyone deserved to dream?

Dante looked at her and shook his head. 'So that is what you call growing up. Maybe you are right, *cara*. We all have to give up our childish dreams sooner or later. We were both young. It was a—what do you call it? A holiday romance. Nothing more. It belongs to the past.'

He picked up his rucksack and hefted it onto his shoulders. 'Your life and mine, they are different. I have seen photographs of you in magazines. Always out at parties, on yachts, at horse racing. You are petted and admired and given your every need. I don't think you would be happy with the simple pleasures in life. A home, a family, children.'

Now he was making her angry. 'You think you know what I want?' She stamped her foot. *How cool and grown up is that?* the detached side of her brain was saying, but she'd had enough of being judged by this man, however much she had once cared about him.

They glared at each other. Then Dante laughed. '*Bellissimo*, you have a temper. You can match an Italian woman any time.' He helped her on with her rucksack. 'We'd better get going. We still have a long way to go before we can make camp.' He glanced over his shoulder at her. 'What is wrong with wanting children and a family and caring for them? It is the way of the world.'

For a second Alice was tempted to grab him by his T-shirt and shake him. Just in time, she managed to restrain the impulse. Thank God, one thing her upbringing had taught her was control.

'We will break again in another two hours. For lunch,' Dante said, before setting off along the track.

Alice smiled. The Italians took their lunch-time seriously. As she continued up the hill she let herself imagine what they would have to eat. No doubt his mother would have organised great food for them. Some sort of pasta dish, perhaps fluffy ravioli stuffed with mushroom and aubergine. Soup first. A minestrone the way only Italians could make it, and then some chicken perhaps, followed by strong coffee.

The fantasy added strength to her legs and kept her preoccupied for the next leg of their climb. When had she last eaten a decent meal? Trying to keep her weight down was a nightmare. If she didn't go to the gym at last three times a week, somehow it crept back on, as if the pounds were just waiting to catch her unawares.

But back then Dante had liked her curves. He had run his hands over her hips, cupping her bottom and whispering his approval.

Stop it! She simply could not allow her thoughts to go in that direction. But it was hopeless. She couldn't stop herself remembering the look in his eyes when they had lain naked on his bed. The way his chest had felt under her fingertips. The silky hair at the base of his abdomen. And he had filled out since then. If anything, he was more muscular, harder, sexier.

Did he have a girlfriend?

Silly question. Of course he did. Someone like him was bound to have a woman in tow.

When Dante stopped by a stream, Alice wasted no time in stripping off her boots and socks and submerging her aching feet in the ice-cold water. She leaned back, savouring the feel of the sun on her face and the cessation of pain as she waited for Dante to serve lunch. He was bound to have a small camping stove in that enormous ruck-sack of his. Surely any minute now the delicious smells of lunch would be drifting across the still air. Alice's stomach rumbled gently. Once her appetite was sated, she'd have no problem with the last leg of the climb. She allowed herself a small smile. If Dante thought he was going to defeat her with this trip, he had miscalculated badly. She couldn't wait to see the approval on his face when she scampered to the top. After lunch.

Where was it?

Looking behind her, she was horrified to see Dante lying flat on a piece of ground, chewing on some bread. There was no little stove boiling away merrily. He took a final bite of his sandwich and closed his eyes. Unbelievably, it seemed as if Dante was having a siesta.

Alice crossed over to where he lay. His eyes were closed and the expression on his face made her heart twist. He looked like a little boy with his long lashes against his cheeks and his beautiful face in repose. The boyish looks of before were replaced by the hard lines and sharp planes of a man. If anything he was far better looking than he had been and she'd found him gorgeous then. There were bracketed lines at the corners of his mouth and eyes that still spoke of a man who liked to laugh. Just not with her.

Suddenly he opened his eyes and Alice found herself locked in his gaze. Her breath caught in her throat as her heart hammered against her ribs. It was so quiet she was convinced he could hear it.

'Er, I just wondered what was for lunch,' she said.

Dante sat up. 'Lunch? Did you not bring food for yourself?' he asked.

Alice flushed under his look of incredulity. 'I

brought a chocolate bar.' She wasn't about to tell him that she planned to keep that for emergencies. Like when she was in her tent, in her sleeping bag, and she couldn't get to sleep and needed some comfort. Oh, no, she wouldn't tell him that.

'A chocolate bar? For two days and one night? Are you crazy?'

'I don't eat much,' was all she could think of to say.

'Dio!' He looked at her as if she was a child who had thrown her supper on the floor. 'You have to eat to do this journey. Didn't you think at all?'

A wave of heat flushed her cheeks. No, she hadn't thought. All her life there had been people who had done that type of thinking for her. They'd always had a cook and other servants. The cook would even prepare picnic lunches if that was what was required. If Alice didn't fancy the food at the university canteen, she would have Maisie make her up some salad to take with her.

'You will have to share with me,' he said. 'We will have to be careful to make it last. But first…'

he held out his hand '…you must give me your chocolate. Everything must be shared.'

Reluctantly Alice retrieved the chocolate from her bag and handed it over. At least it was a family-sized bar. On the other hand, seeing the size of it, he was bound to think her greedy. To top it all, the bar was beginning to melt. God, she felt about five years old.

Dante cut a couple of slices of bread with his penknife and slapped some ham in the middle, before handing it to her. Although it wasn't quite the three-course feast she had been expecting, it still tasted good. It would have tasted better if she hadn't been eating it with the dry dust of embarrassment clogging her throat.

Once more they set off, a mortified, limping Alice feeling more and more like a broken woman. All she could do was think about what an idiot she must look to Dante. Surely he would refuse to let her go to Africa now. The thought was almost unbearable. But the trip wasn't over yet—not by a long chalk. She still had time to show Dante that she could do anything she put her mind to—even if she wasn't at all sure right now that she could.

CHAPTER THREE

DANTE marched on, trying not to think about who was walking behind him.

It had been a crazy idea to even suggest Alice come on this hike. He knew that now. The truth was he had known it the moment he had issued the challenge.

Then why had he? One look at Alice back in the ballroom had told him she had changed. No, that wasn't right. She hadn't changed—it was just that the woman he had met in Italy wasn't the real Alice. The one in the ballroom, dressed up with jewels—the one in the pictures—that was the real Alice and he didn't know her at all. She was no different from Natalia and it was good that he'd found it out before it was too late. *Dio*, he had been stupid to think she was any different. Like Natalia she wanted a life where money and

status was what was important. After the charity
dinner, when he had known she was coming to
Africa, he had looked her up on the internet as
soon as he'd returned to Italy. There were hundreds of photos of her, at film premieres, leaving
nightclubs, at parties. Sometimes with her father
by her side, sometimes with friends, too often
with that man she had called Peter.

Not that what she did was anything to do with
him. He shouldn't even be thinking about her.
But like a fly trapped in a room he couldn't stop
his memories buzzing around his head.

Apart from her physical appearance, she was
much thinner. He had liked Alice's curves.
Somewhere along the way, her smile, the sparkle
in her eyes had almost been extinguished. Her
skin, once flushed with sun and happiness, was
almost translucent; now there were dark shadows
under her eyes that no amount of make-up could
hide. But it was those light green eyes that had
given him the worst shock. They were almost
dead. She'd looked so unhappy when he'd seen
her in London that he'd been angry. He'd wanted

to gather her into his arms and take her away, back to Italy, to bring a glow back to her cheeks, to see that smile that lit her up from inside. But he couldn't. She had run away from him. She wasn't his. She had never been his.

He kicked a stone with the tip of his boot, watching with satisfaction as it skidded away into the undergrowth.

The truth was, he hadn't expected her to agree to come to Italy and do the hike. Even when she'd insisted on coming, he'd never thought she'd make it halfway up the mountain, let alone be traipsing after him like a determined bloodhound.

When he'd seen her standing outside the hostel, he'd almost laughed. She had been dressed as if she were modelling the latest outdoor gear for some fancy department store. Those boots. He could almost have seen his face in them.

He'd known she'd get a blister. What he hadn't expected had been for her to suffer in silence until he had noticed. Maybe he had underestimated her? Perhaps the Alice he had known in Italy wasn't completely dead and gone?

But then, when she had looked around for her lunch as if expecting a team of caterers to appear and set it out on a table for her, his reservations had come roaring back. It was just as well he was used to planning for the unexpected and had taken extra provisions. Not that he had told her that. Let her sweat it out for a while. He grinned to himself when he thought back to her handing over her chocolate. Anyone would have thought she was handing over her life. And the way embarrassment had coloured her cheeks. For the first time he had seen a glimpse of the beautiful, sexy woman she had been. Not this mannequin look she preferred.

After she'd left Italy, and he had found out the truth about her, he had sworn he would never fall in love with another woman. Twice he had been wrong about a woman. First with Natalia. Then with Alice. Never again. So why, then, was he torturing himself by having her here? Hadn't he spent the last year trying to forget her? She was a shallow, spoilt actress and he had to remember that. She had deceived him once and wasn't to be trusted. Whatever happened, he must never forget that. Whoever the real Alice was, she would never be part of his life.

The sun was sinking in the sky by the time they made it to their camping place a few hundred metres below the top of the mountain. They would finish the climb the next morning and the rest of the day would be taken up with making their way back. Dante had picked this place to pitch their tent because he knew it was the last flat piece of ground before the summit. He had done this climb many times before. It was easy for him to do it in a single day, but then again he was fitter than most men. And a lot fitter than Alice, who had collapsed in a heap at his feet.

'Just a minute's rest, please,' she groaned. 'Then I promise I'll help put up the tents.'

Tents? Did she really think he would bring two when one would do? He had planned to sleep outside but as the sky darkened and thick clouds scudded overhead he knew that a storm was on the way. It would be foolish for him to sleep in the rain.

Heat burned low in his stomach at the thought of sleeping inches away from Alice. Maybe he should sleep outside? Let the rain cool his libido? But those were the thoughts of a weak man. Not a man who was used to denial.

'There is only one tent,' he told Alice. 'And there is a storm on the way. I'm afraid we are going to have to share it. But don't worry. At least you will be warm and dry.'

He almost laughed out loud at the flash of alarm in her eyes.

'You will be perfectly safe, I promise you. There is a little waterfall over there…' he pointed off to one side '…with a stream at the bottom. If you want, you can wash and I will put up the tent and make us some coffee.'

The thought of coffee brought some light back into her eyes.

'I can help put up the tent, if you want.'

Dante shook his head. She had been through enough for one day. Besides, he suspected that her help with the tent would mean wasted time erecting it, and as a fork of lightning split the sky, time wasn't what they had.

'No, but you can make the coffee if you like.' He pulled the small stove out of his rucksack as well as a pan. He had more bread, ham and cheese for their dinner. It was what he always took whenever he hiked. It was easy to transport and full of the calories they needed. 'Perhaps you could fetch some water from the stream first? Once it starts raining we won't be able to heat anything on it.'

It seemed the thought of not having hot coffee was enough to energise Alice. Carrying the plastic water container he gave her, she set off while he started on putting up the tent.

It only took five minutes to get the tent sorted but by then the sky had darkened considerably and there was an ominous roll of thunder not very far away. Dante knew it wouldn't be long before the skies opened.

He finished organising the camp and sat back on his heels to wait for Alice. God, he needed a coffee. Perhaps he should go and see what had happened to her? What if she had managed to get herself into trouble? The thought brought him to his feet. It wasn't really as if very much could happen but with Alice, who knew? He would check, just to be on the safe side.

He marched across to the part of the river where she had been heading. As far as he remembered, there was no steep slope where she could slip and the river wasn't deep.

Sure enough, there was the water container filled and set down next to the bank. But that wasn't all. There was a neat pile of jeans, walking boots and T-shirt. Pulse hammering in his temple, his eyes tracked along the water until he saw her. She had stripped off, and like some sea sprite had waded out into the middle of the river. Unable to move, he watched mesmerised as she dipped her head under water and came up rapidly, gasping from the cold. Her hair steamed down, covering her shoulders. He could make out her narrow waist and the swell of her breasts.

Sweet mother of God.

She was beautiful and sexy as hell. Why had she come back into his life?

Why hadn't he met another woman who could set him on fire even a fraction as much as this one?

And what was he going to do about it?

The first drops of rain were starting to fall when Alice arrived back at the camp with the water. God, that dip in the stream had been good. Now that she was clean and cool she could face just about anything. Not having anticipated her impromptu bath, she hadn't taken a towel down to the stream with her. Although she had plaited her wet hair, the water streamed down her back and over her T-shirt.

Dante glanced at her and his eyes darkened.

She followed his eyes and whipped her arms across her chest. The white T-shirt was clinging to her body, the water making the thin material transparent. She hadn't bothered putting her underwear back on and she knew that her breasts must be perfectly visible to Dante. Blushing furiously, she kept her voice light.

'Sorry I took so long. I couldn't resist cooling off in the stream. Don't worry, I took the water from further up, where it comes over the rocks, so it should be safe to drink.'

Dante only grunted in reply. What was up with the man now?

He filled a pot with water and set it on the small camping stove to heat. 'It's going to rain soon and there isn't enough space in the tent to cook. I will cut us some bread if you can make the coffee. Is this okay with you?'

The tension emanating from him was almost palpable. What had she done wrong now? Okay, so she should have thought to pack some food, but it wasn't exactly a shooting offence, was it?

The sky continued to darken as they ate their meal. Alice felt a pang of guilt. Dante was a big man and here she was eating half his rations. He ate like he did everything—with total concentration and without saying anything. Alice discovered she was ravenous too and was more than happy to concentrate on her food.

Besides, she could think of nothing to say that wouldn't sound defensive or trite.

After they'd finished eating, he set another pot on the stove for more coffee. Almost as soon as he had poured them both a mug, it started to rain.

Quickly she helped him pack away the dishes and then they scooted inside the tent.

It was too small, Alice thought nervously. There was no room for them to sit without touching each other and it was only…she glanced at her watch…seven o'clock. How on earth was she going to get through the hours until she fell asleep in such close proximity to him?

But if being shoehorned into the tent together bothered Dante, he gave no indication of it. He passed Alice her sleeping bag before unrolling his and placing it on the ground.

'I'll leave you to get changed,' he said, and before she could reply he was out of the tent.

As Alice struggled out of her clothes and into the jogging pants and T-shirt she had brought to sleep in, her mind was in overdrive. What would Dante sleep in? Somehow she couldn't see him in pyjamas. At least they had their own sleeping bags and if she could just keep her mind off the thought of him, perhaps she'd make it through the night. The sound of rain was like popcorn popping on the canvas.

Just as Alice was getting settled the zipper of the tent alerted her to Dante's return. He must have gone down to the river too, or else it was raining harder than she thought. He had taken off his shirt and his torso was sprinkled with tiny drops of water. She watched mesmerised as a single drop snaked its way across the scar on his shoulder before travelling down towards the top of his jeans.

Oh, my God.

Her nerve endings were thrumming like a still vibrating guitar string. Little explosions of lust were doing things to her abdomen that hadn't been done since she'd been with Dante—and Peter certainly hadn't done them. Ever.

She must have been staring because he turned

and looked at her. Their eyes locked and Alice went shooting back to their last night together.

He smiled wryly and she knew he'd been remembering too. His hands went to the top button of his jeans and Alice took a sharp intake of breath. What was he going to do? Pick up where they'd left off a year ago?

He paused and lifted an eyebrow at her. 'I'm warning you, I am naked under these.' Amusement threaded his voice. He unbuttoned his jeans and started easing them down over his hips.

Alice snapped her eyes closed. She heard his laugh as his jeans landed on the ground with a thud. Then there was a rustle as he eased into his sleeping bag. Alice was almost rigid. She could smell his particular scent, and it was driving her crazy. Why shouldn't she make a move? What could it hurt? They were both adults.

Tentatively she opened her eyes. Couldn't he hear her heart beating even above the sound of the rain on the canvas roof of the tent? She propped herself on an elbow.

His face in repose was like a statue. Severe and unrelenting. Except for the laughter lines around his eyes. Once he had laughed often. Once she had been the one to make him laugh.

'Dante,' she whispered. No reply. She tried again. 'Dante,' she said more loudly.

Still no response. She leaned closer. His breathing was deep and rhythmical. He was asleep. He was less than four inches away from her and he had fallen asleep. Alice was glad there was no one to see how that even the tips of her ears were burning. So much for thinking that Dante had even the slightest vestige of feeling left for her. Whatever else had happened over the last months, that had clearly gone.

The day's unaccustomed exercise took its toll and eventually Alice fell asleep. Some time in the middle of the night she was awoken by the sound of snuffling and grunting. Her heart pounding, she lay rigid with fear. What was it? Was it a wolf, one of the wild boars Dante had mentioned? The sound came again. This time it was closer, definitely some animal that was pushing at the canvas of the tent.

She jerked upright and, leaning over, touched Dante on the shoulder.

'Dante, wake up!'

It was too dark for her to see if he was awake and she was about to call his name again when his arm slid around her shoulders and pulled her close.

'Bella?' he murmured. His hand was in her hair and her face was against his bare chest. His smell, the scent she remembered so well, the feel of his skin against hers, the secure feeling of being wrapped in his arms and held, relaxed her immediately.

'Cara.' His breath was a whisper on her skin and a flame of desire shot through her body, pooling in her abdomen.

She turned her face towards his and his mouth found hers. His lips, the taste of his mouth sent her thoughts spinning out of control.

Suddenly his hands reached for her shoulders and pushed her away.

'God, what kind of game are you playing?' His voice was rough.

She felt as if she'd been slapped. She was glad the darkness hid her mortification.

'I was just trying to wake you,' she muttered. 'I heard something outside. I didn't expect to be accosted.' She was simply going to ignore the fact she had kissed him back.

Thankfully the strange sounds from outside were still audible, although now they were far less scary than being kissed by Dante.

He laughed shortly. 'It is only some animal. A small deer perhaps, maybe a wild boar. Nothing to be frightened of.' There was a long pause. 'Go back to sleep, Alice.'

The next time she woke it was to the sounds of the birds and the smell of coffee on the breeze.

Dante was hunched over the camping stove, whistling to himself. She smothered a groan as she walked over to him. Every muscle in her body ached.

Dante looked up. His eyes crinkled at the corners. '*Buongiorno*. How did you sleep?'

Like the princess and the pea. But it wasn't the hard ground that had kept her awake. She could hardly tell him that after the animal incident she had lain awake, her body fizzing with the memory of his hard body against hers. The brief touch of his hands on her shoulders. She couldn't tell him that her whole body had ached to be back in his arms. As for the humiliation of being removed from his arms and put aside, *that* would stay with her for a long time. Whatever had been between them in Italy was clearly a distant and not very pleasant memory to him now.

Dante handed her a mug and she took it gratefully wrapping her hands around it to warm her hands. A fine mist lay over the hills and it was considerably cooler up in the mountains than it had been in the city.

'How are your feet?' Dante asked. He set his mug on the ground and crouched in front of her. He lifted her foot onto his lap and examined her heel. 'Is it very sore?' he asked.

Not half as painful as the feel of his cool hands on her skin and the memories it brought flooding back.

'I'll be fine,' she said, and yanked her foot from his grasp. His lips twitched and, damn the man, that was definitely a smile she saw in his eyes. It was all right for him. He had slept like a baby the whole night. Clearly completely unaffected by her presence only inches away.

'How long until we get to the top?' she asked.

'Two hours, maybe three. It depends how fast we move.'

'And back down?'

'It will be quicker than coming up. We have to be down before it's dark.' He passed her a biscuit. 'Eat this,' he said. 'It is breakfast.'

Alice eyed the biscuit with disappointment. Was that it? What about her chocolate?

'We will have the chocolate when we reach the top,' he said, reading her mind. 'It will be your reward.'

But when they finally reached the top two hours later, the surprised look in Dante's eyes was all the reward she needed. As was the view. It stretched away into the distance, the peaks of the mountains still topped with snow.

Although they made short work of the descent, Alice was relieved when they finally arrived back at the foot of the mountain.

'Come,' he said. 'We will go to a *trattoria* nearby in the village and have some hot food. I don't know about you but I am hungry.'

Alice tried not to show her embarrassment. He was bound to be starving after sharing his food with her. She just wished he hadn't felt the need to remind her.

She jumped into his car and in typical Dante fashion they sped back down the narrow roads as if he was trying to set some personal speed record. Alice was relieved when he drew up outside a pretty rose-covered *trattoria* with tables outside under the shade of a loggia.

'So have I passed?' she asked when they were settled with their pasta and coffee.

Dante smiled that slow sexy smile of his.

'Okay, so I was wrong. You are stronger than

you look. But I have to warn you this is easy compared to what you will experience in Africa. The heat for one thing, and I hope you don't mind spiders and snakes too much. I think animals frighten you.' His smile widened.

'Spiders! Snakes!' Alice shuddered. 'Poisonous ones?' She had no sooner survived wild boar and wolves and now he was talking about creepy-crawlies.

'Some,' Dante replied, 'but there are usually only one or two deaths a year. You have to remember to check your shoes for scorpions every morning. Otherwise you should be all right.'

Only one or two deaths a year. Even that sounded way too much. Alice stiffened her spine. If other people could cope well, so could she. As for her behaviour in the tent last night, well, if he hadn't mentioned wolves it would never have occurred to her to be frightened. So that was that. It was all his fault she had been scared witless.

'*Bene*, I will take you to a hotel.' His face relaxed into a real smile. 'I think you might like that, *sì*? And then tomorrow you can take a plane back to London.'

Alice's heart plunged to her shiny walking boots.

'What? After all I did? I climbed that bloody mountain without a murmur, well, not much of one anyway. I did everything you asked. So I will not go back! No way. I am going to Africa whether you like it or not.'

Dante looked bemused. 'I thought you'd want to go to your home for a few days. Have some rest. Maybe have another chance to think about coming to Africa?'

'I've not changed my mind. I'm going and the sooner the better.'

'*Bene.* You have kept your part of the deal, and so I will keep mine.'

CHAPTER FOUR

As THE truck bounced its way along the rutted dirt track, Alice felt every jolt in her aching body. She was tired and grouchy and, she had to admit, nervous. So far they had been travelling for almost twenty-four hours and the journey wasn't over yet. They had flown to Khartoum and from there they had been picked up by a truck that would take them, along with supplies for the camp, the rest of the way. A distance of several hundred kilometres.

The driver was an older Italian by the name of Luigi. He and Dante seemed to know each other well. The three of them sat in the front, the back being loaded with supplies for the camp, except for a small area that as Dante had explained had been left free so that they could take turns stretching out for a sleep. They were squashed together and the sensation of the hard muscles of Dante's thigh against hers was making it difficult for Alice to concentrate.

Luigi had explained that he would be driving through the night. The camp was waiting for the supplies and he didn't want to waste any time stopping except for essential meal and toilet breaks.

As Dante and Luigi chatted in Italian about football and motorbikes, Alice stared out the window, trying to ignore the feel of Dante's body pressed next to hers. The landscape was changing, turning ever more arid and hotter the further into the interior they drove.

She slid a glance at Dante. With her he was quiet, almost taciturn, whereas with Luigi he was relaxed and the smile she had loved when they had first met was frequent and easy.

Would he ever smile at her like that again?

She wanted him to.

They broke their journey to stop for lunch at a roadside hut. Luigi and Dante tucked into their stew with gusto, but it was all Alice could do to take a few mouthfuls, even if it was delicious. Her stomach was knotted. Was Dante right? Would she be unable to cope with the conditions? But the thought of returning home, tail between her legs, was more than she could bear. She would cope. After all, she had made it up that mountain and back down again. And what about spending more time with Dante? How would it be, seeing him every day, knowing he no longer even liked her?

When it got dark, Luigi stopped the truck and climbed into the back, letting Dante take over the driving. Now it was just the two of them she felt shy again. She wanted to tell him why she had left, but what could she say? Nevertheless she had to try.

She cleared her throat.

'Are you seeing someone?' she asked tentatively.

Dante looked at her. In the semi-darkness she couldn't read his expression.

'No,' he said briefly.

Despite her anxiety, Alice couldn't help a small

surge of happiness. He wasn't with anyone. Not that it should make any difference to her.

'I'm sorry,' she said.

His mouth twitched. 'Why are you sorry? I'm not. I have a good life and I can please myself.'

'I didn't mean I was sorry you're not with someone,' Alice said hastily. 'I meant I was sorry about what happened.' She shifted in her seat. 'I shouldn't have left without saying goodbye. It was wrong.'

Once again he shrugged. 'You did what you had to do.' He slid a look at her. 'As you said, you were young. It was just an affair. It didn't mean anything.'

Was that how he saw it? Just an affair? Had she spent all this time agonising over what might have been when it had meant so little to him? What a fool she'd been. What an innocent, gullible fool.

'But,' he said after a moment's silence, 'there was no reason to lie to me.' There was no mistaking the contempt in his voice.

'I didn't lie. I just didn't tell you the truth.'

'It is the same thing.'

'You've seen how I live. Those weeks in Italy were the first time I was ever able to just be me. All my life I have done what I was supposed to do. I could never be certain that people wanted to be with me because they genuinely liked me, or because of who I was.' Now, that sounded pathetic. She knew she wasn't explaining herself very well.

'I never imagined for one moment that I would fall…I mean, that our relationship would get so serious so quickly,' she rushed on. 'When you asked me to stay longer, I wanted to, but it was impossible. I had a duty at home. I know it probably doesn't make sense to you, but…' She let the words hang in the air. But what? She could hardly tell him she'd been falling for him. Not when she clearly had meant so little to him.

Dante raised an eyebrow. 'I can see now, the idea of you staying was crazy. I'm sure you were longing to get back to your comfortable life.'

'It wasn't the money,' Alice said, exasperated. 'It was just I knew I had to get back to my life before…' Once more she tailed off. There was no way she could explain. But she had to make him see that her time in Italy, her time with him, had changed her. 'In the last few months I've been helping raise money for the charity, but I know that still isn't enough. That's why I'm here. I don't want to be on the outside any more, sitting in my ivory tower, not really knowing what life is like in the real world. I know I should have been honest with you, but at least I see *my* faults.'

'At least now we both know that it would have been a mistake, you staying in Italy,' Dante said ignoring the emphasis she had given the pronoun. He reached over and switched on the radio, making it clear that the conversation was over. As the Italian newscaster read out the news, Alice leaned her head against the worn leather of the passenger seat and closed her eyes.

Dante kept his eyes fixed on the road in front of him.

He replayed the conversation in his head. She had lied to him, there was no getting away from that, but was there some truth in what she said? He hadn't thought twice about asking her to stay longer. Had he truly thought about her? He'd been taken by surprise by the intensity of his feelings for her and selfishly he had just wanted her to stay with him.

He slid her a look. She was still beautiful, even if some of the light had gone out of her.

Despite his determination to forget about her, he'd never managed to. He remembered everything about her. The way the dimples appeared in the corners of her mouth when she smiled, the little gap between her two front teeth, the silky feel of her skin under his fingers, the smell of her perfume that she still wore, the memory of his face buried in her golden hair when they had made love, the way she had rested her head on his chest afterwards and drawn lazy circles on his chest.

Dio. She had driven him crazy in Italy. He had been in danger of falling in love with her.

And he'd thought she'd cared about him too. Not just thought, he'd been sure.

But he'd been wrong. She had slipped away like a thief in the night. He stifled a moan. Whatever she said about why she hadn't stayed was just an excuse.

He had his work and that was all that mattered. There had been more than one woman since Alice, only somehow they had never felt right in his arms.

Why had Alice pretended? Because it had amused her. Like a game, where she could pretend? But as soon as the game had turned serious, she had run.

It had hurt his pride. That was all.

No doubt as soon as she got to the camp, she would run again. As soon as he had seen her again, he had instantly understood the life she lived. Women like Alice couldn't cope with the conditions. He would give her twenty-four hours. Maybe forty-eight, but no more. Then she'd be begging to call her father to take her home.

But he had to admit she had surprised him. If he'd thought that she'd take one look at the hostel he had booked for her and run, he'd been mistaken. Then she had done the climb. He smiled, remembering the challenge in her eyes when he'd picked her up. She'd been so proud of her new boots, and had battled on despite the inevitable blister. She hadn't given up. Not even when he'd tried to make it as difficult as possible for her. And the first time she'd been in Italy the day they'd met, and there had been the accident with the child, Alice had been scared, but she'd stayed calm. Maybe he had underestimated her? Perhaps she had grown up in the time they had been apart. Nevertheless, the camp was something else again. This would be much harder for her than a mere walk and although she had been good with Sofia, the children she would see at the camp were something else entirely.

He switched off the radio. In the silence he could hear her breathing had become regular, deeper. She had fallen asleep. Slowly she tipped sideways until her head rested on his shoulder. She wriggled as she tried to get more comfortable. Then finally she sighed, laid her head in his lap and curled her knees up on the seat. A small sigh of satisfaction escaped as she made herself comfortable.

He couldn't stop his hand from stroking the hair away from where it had fallen across her face. The familiar silky feel of it sent a shock of memory to his pelvis. Why had she come back into his life when he had begun to forget about her?

CHAPTER FIVE

ALICE opened her eyes and blinked. Where was she? There was something hard yet soft under her head and a familiar scent of aftershave. God, she had fallen asleep and somehow her head had come to rest in Dante's lap. She bolted upright.

'I'm sorry,' she said. 'I didn't mean to do that.'

Dawn light was filtering through the windows and now she could see Dante's face clearly.

He looked tired, which was hardly surprising as he must have driven through the night.

'It's okay. You needed to sleep. We should be there soon.'

It was intensely hot inside the truck. Alice now knew how a chicken in an oven must feel like. It wasn't just the heat, it was the humidity and most of all the dust. Her clothes were sticking to her, a rivulet of sweat was trickling between her breasts and her hair was hanging in rats' tails.

After so long on the road, Alice was looking forward to arriving at the camp. Her eyes were scratchy from lack of sleep and she was dying to wash the dirt out of her hair under a cool shower. But, despite her physical discomfort, she couldn't remember the last time she had been so excited by something. Excited *and* scared. Would she really be able to cope? Dante was right. Working in these conditions wasn't something she was used to, but she would give it everything she had.

The lorry stopped its jolting as they came to a halt.

Dante leaped out and came over to the passenger side to open the door for Alice. He held out a hand and helped her jump out. In contrast to his loose-limbed movements, her limbs were aching and she hobbled on her heels for the first few steps. Then she took her first look around.

She sucked in a breath, horrified. Tents and other makeshift shelters stretched for almost as far as the eye could see. People, there must be hundreds of them, were sitting on the ground, watching with detached boredom. There were donkeys and goats huddling together, and some of the women were milking the goats. Other women were carrying firewood and water on their heads.

Alice swallowed hard. Whatever she'd imagined, it hadn't been this. How were they supposed to look after so many people? Where had they all come from? Where were they going?

A crowd of excited children rushed over to them and faces beamed up at her. Dante had almost been swallowed up by them and he swung two into his arms. The noise was deafening. Alice was disoriented and dismayed. Perhaps everyone had been right. She didn't belong here.

An older woman with short grey hair came towards them with her hand outstretched.

'Dante, it's good to have you back. We've missed you.'

He grinned broadly and swept her up in a bear hug. 'Linda. How are you?' He rattled something off in Italian Alice couldn't follow. Linda laughed and turned to Alice.

'You must be Alice. We heard someone was coming from the charity to see conditions for themselves. I can't tell you how pleased we are to have you both.' Despite the genuine warmth of her greeting, Linda eyed Alice and her shoes doubtfully and flicked a glance at Dante. Alice knew that despite her dusty crumpled appearance, Linda was taking in the Hermès scarf she had wrapped around her neck, the designer jeans and blouse, her *totally* inappropriate shoes and her manicured nails. She probably guessed that what Alice was wearing would pay for food for one of the refugees for a year. Alice cringed. She knew Linda was wondering whether Alice was going to be a help or a hindrance. Tough. She was here now and she would do whatever she could, until her time was up.

'Alice, this is Linda, senior nurse and camp organiser,' Dante introduced the older woman.

'A new assignment of vaccines has arrived and it means all hands on deck,' Linda continued, after shaking hands with Alice. 'I'm afraid I'm going to have to steal Dante straight away. But you must be tired, Alice. I'm sure you'd like a rest.'

Alice shook her head. 'No, I'm fine, really. I can get started straight away.'

Linda looked at her with approval. 'That's my girl. I'll just show you where you'll be sleeping and you can dump your stuff there and freshen up.'

Before Alice could reach for her bag, Dante had hefted it onto his shoulder along with his.

'How's it been?' he asked Linda, leaving Alice to follow behind with the excited children. A small hand slipped into hers.

'Not too bad. But malaria season will be here shortly. I'd feel happier if we had everyone vaccinated against everything else before it truly arrives. Once the rains come there is no guarantee of getting more supplies.'

As they walked, Alice glanced around at the place which would be her home for the next few weeks. Most of the shelters were little more than cardboard boxes or small huts made from sticks and bits of plastic. A child wearing a ragged T-shirt three sizes too big for him skipped along, pulling a hand-made truck made from scrap metal. Although the film Dante had shown the night of the dinner had shown all of this, the reality was so much worse.

'How many others work here?' she asked.

Linda swung around. 'Well there's me and two other nurses, Hanuna and Dixie, Pascale, the other doctor, and Costa our aid worker. As you might be able to tell, we're a mixed bunch from all over the world. Some of the residents of the camp who have been here for a while help out too, so we're not too badly off. Lydia, one of the doctors, has left on leave already. She'll be coming back when Dante goes. So what's that? Six, and with you seven—apart from the residents.'

Six! Linda had only been polite to include Alice in the numbers. And there were hundreds, if not thousands, in the camp.

They stopped next to a tent and Linda opened

a flap. 'This will be your home for the next few weeks, Alice.'

Alice's home was a tent with four camp beds and a couple of steel tables with a dirt floor. Although Dante had warned her that facilities at the camp were basic, Alice had imagined a little house with a small room to herself. Not this. She tried to hide her dismay.

'You share with me and the two nurses,' Linda explained. 'You have Lydia's bed while she is away.' She turned to Dante 'You're in with Costa—I think you worked with him before at one of the other camps? The same tent as last time. Alice, I'll leave you to unpack and settle in. I'll be back in a minute to introduce you to everyone and show you around.' She turned to Dante. 'No doubt you'll want to get stuck in straight away, Dante?'

He nodded. 'I'll catch up with you later, Alice.' He waved his hand and Alice was left alone.

Stunned and dismayed, she forced herself to unpack her bag, placing her belongings neatly on the hanging shelf beside her bed. Then she tested the bed. It was narrow, squeaked, had little give, and was only marginally better than a sleeping bag on the ground. Above it, suspended by a metal hook, was a filmy piece of gauze. That would be the mosquito net Dante had told her about. He'd emphasised that she had to remember to use it every night to keep the insects at bay.

Now that she had unpacked she wondered what to do. She was feeling hotter by the minute as the canvas of the tent was doing nothing to alleviate the heat—quite the opposite. Alice wished she had asked Linda where the showers were. There was a bucket of water on the table and she splashed her face and neck. The water was lukewarm but Alice felt cooler. Linda had said she'd come back for her, but Alice was too wound up to wait. She changed into a fresh T-shirt and replaced her shoes with flats before making her way out of the tent. Bewildered, she looked around. Where would she find Dante and Linda? Shielding her eyes from the sun, she noticed a large canvas structure a few metres away. Sitting outside, holding children in their arms, were a number of women. She went over to where a small table had been set up outside the tent. Linda was drawing liquid into a syringe while Dante was examining a little girl.

Linda looked up as Alice approached.

'Hello, there. I was about to come and get you, but I got caught up.' She smiled an apology. 'I thought you'd take the chance to have a rest.'

'I couldn't. I'd rather get stuck in, if that's okay with you.'

Linda smiled briefly. 'We can do with all the help we can get. Give me a minute until I give this jab.'

A mother was holding her child as Linda gave the injection into the child's arm. The little face crumpled for a moment, but the toddler didn't cry.

'The first thing we do, after we register the people who come here and sort them out with the basics, is vaccinate. We need to do that so that we don't bring disease into the camp. If you really mean it about being willing to help, maybe you can start in registration.'

'I'm happy to do whatever I can,' Alice replied. Although she had no idea what registration involved, it didn't sound too complicated and it would give her something to do. Anything to keep her mind off the situation here at the camp could only be good, particularly if it kept her away from Dante. Perhaps after helping out she could take notes for her report to the charity. The sooner people knew about the awful situation here, the better.

'I'll take you across, but I'll be a few minutes yet. There's still quite a few people waiting for their jabs.' Linda dropped the used syringe in a sealed container and prepared another as the queue moved forward.

Alice shuffled her feet, feeling like a nuisance.

Dante finished examining his patient and strode over to Linda.

'I need to admit the youngest child and mother to the ward. The girl is severely malnourished. There is an older child with them. Someone should keep an eye on him while I sort out the rest of the family.'

'I can do that,' Alice offered. 'I'm not doing anything else at the moment.'

Dante looked doubtful for a second, as if he was certain she couldn't be trusted with even that small task. Then he seemed to make up his mind and smiled. 'The boy is about eight. He doesn't speak any English. He needs to go and collect firewood. Will you go with him? He knows where to go.'

'That sounds easy enough,' Alice said, becoming a little exasperated. She wasn't a complete idiot, no matter what Dante thought.

Dante beckoned the boy across. Alice was shocked. He was wearing a T-shirt that had more holes than cloth, below which two skinny bare legs protruded. Dante had said he was eight. He looked closer to five.

'Hassan is responsible for making a fire to cook on tonight. He will stay with another family until his mother is well enough to look after him, but will be expected to pull his weight.'

Hassan was staring at her with listless eyes.

Alice held out her hand for him to take but he shook his head shyly.

'If you can help him gather wood, that will be a big help. If we had more space and more beds, I would admit him too. He needs feeding up almost as much as his sister.'

Dante said a few words to Hassan who nodded and, casting a glance at Alice, set off towards a cluster of trees in the distance.

Alice followed behind him, stepping carefully while keeping an eye out for snakes. This little boy should be being looked after, not made to work. It wasn't right. None of this was right.

Eventually they came to a clearing amongst a number of acacia trees. There were several women and small children bending and foraging for fallen branches. They looked up when they noticed Alice and said something she couldn't understand. One of them handed her a basket with straps attached.

Bewildered, Alice watched as Hassan collected broken branches and deftly tied them into a bundle, before dropping them into her basket.

After a few more minutes he had collected another bundle, which he tied onto his back. He looked at Alice with his solemn eyes. He seemed to be waiting for her to do something. Noticing her hesitation, one of the women approached Alice and lifted the now full basket of wood, indicating that she should slip it on her back.

Alice didn't know whether she felt more ridiculous for not knowing that that was what she was supposed to do, or for almost crumbling under the weight of the wood. As she blew out her cheeks and groaned, Hassan gave his first small smile.

She followed him back up the path, almost staggering under the weight of the basket. She was glad she had at least swapped her heels for flat shoes. She could only imagine how ridiculous she would have looked teetering along under the weight of the firewood in her narrow heels.

As they passed by the tent where Dante and Linda were working Dante looked up. Catching sight of her, his face broke into a wide grin. At least he found something amusing, she grumbled to herself. Personally she failed to see anything funny in this whole sorry, desperate scenario. It was all much worse than she could have possibly imagined. The painful plight of the refugees, the conditions in the camp, the fact that the small child carrying his load of wood so determinedly in front of her when he should be being cared for himself all made her want to cry. Yet Dante was smiling.

As soon as she and Hassan had given their load of firewood to the family he would be staying with, Alice went back to find Linda again. When she looked behind her it was to find Hassan following close on her heels. She had assumed he'd stay with the family but it seemed he had been told to stick with her. He stopped and stared at her. When she smiled at him, he started walking again.

By the time she and her shadow returned to where Linda and Dante had been working, Linda still had a large queue of patients. Dante was writing something onto cards.

'I'm sorry, Alice. I still can't take you. I'll be

another half an hour at the most. Perhaps you want to get a drink or something while you wait?'

Dante stood up from the table where he'd been writing.

'I'll take her across if you like. I'm finished here for the moment and want to check up that there's no one Kadiga needs me to see,' he said.

'Would you, Dante?' As she talked Linda kept on working. 'I'm really sorry to neglect you, Alice, but I'll catch up with you later.'

'Please,' Alice said. 'Don't worry about me. I can look after myself.'

Alice caught the glance Dante and Linda shared and glared at Dante. Hadn't she just fetched wood? Even though it was probably the first physical work she had done in her life. And if her load hadn't been much bigger than Hassan's, it was still an achievement.

'C'mon,' Dante said. 'I'll take you to registration and introduce you to some of the others.'

Alice held out her hand for Hassan. Once more he shook his head but padded after her in his bare feet.

'How are his sister and mother?' Alice asked.

'The mother should be all right after a day or two's rest and proper food, but I'm worried about the little girl. Sometimes when they are so malnourished it is difficult for us to find a vein to put in a drip and this is the case with Samah. I've had to put a line into her neck. Just here.'

He touched Alice on the collar bone and a sizzle of heat ran down her spine.

'And will that work?'

'I don't know. I hope so. All we can do is wait.' His eyes were hooded, the set of his mouth grim.

As they walked towards the perimeter of the camp, men and women looked up lethargically to watch their progress. The women far outnumbered the men.

'Where are all the men?' Alice asked.

'Most of them left the villages some time ago for the city to try and find work to support their families. The women and children wait as long as they can for them to come back. When they can't wait any longer, when they get ill or run out of food they come to us. If they came sooner we might be able to do more for more of them, but none of them want to leave their villages until their men return. Not unless they have to.'

It was a world Alice had no knowledge of. It was one thing hearing about it on the radio, or even in Dante's presentation, quite another being here and seeing it firsthand. Not for the first time, Alice felt ashamed of how she had led her life up until now. Never again would she think of what was happening in the wider world with no more than a passing stab of sympathy.

'It can be tough.' Dante continued. 'We'll over-work you, I'm afraid. But you must tell us when you need to rest. It's too easy for us just to keep going, but it's not healthy. The people here need us to stay fit. After I show you where we register the refugees, I'll show you the hospital and the clinic.'

'How many people are here?' Alice asked. She felt a small hand slip into hers. Hassan glanced up at her before looking down at his feet again. She gave his hand a little squeeze. If she was shocked and out of her depth, how much worse did he feel?

'Not too many at the moment. This is a new camp and pretty well organised. There's one a little way up the road. They have twenty thousand. When we reach that number we set up another camp. The one up the road has surgical facilities. But more people are coming here every day. I suspect it won't be long before we reach our maximum.'

Twenty thousand! In one camp! It was unbelievable. Unacceptable. Overwhelming. Alice knew with a gut-wrenching certainty she was out of her depth. Coming here had been a crazy idea. What had she been thinking? What was she trying to prove? And to whom?

Dante stopped in front of a large khaki tent.

'This is where we register everyone. I know it might seem a bureaucratic process, but it's necessary. Apart from making sure everyone has equal access to food and other supplies, we also take as much information from them as possible. Many have become separated from their families and this way there is a chance that we can reunite families eventually.'

There was a queue of about fifty people, mostly women with children waiting outside. Alice was horrified to see how thin and malnourished the children looked and how tired and exhausted the mothers were.

Dante must have noticed Alice's look of dismay.

'Some of them have walked hundreds of miles to get here. But at least they are here now. We give them food and shelter, treat their medical conditions and in time most get better.'

'Most?' Alice's mouth was dry and it wasn't just from the dust.

Dante's expression softened. 'Some don't make it. You should be prepared for that.'

Dante introduced her to Kadiga, a cheerful woman with a white scarf wrapped around her head. 'Kadiga has been with us since the camp opened. She was a librarian in her old life. As well as speaking English and Arabic, she speaks, or at least understands, most of the African dialects so she is best able to take all the details.

Once she's done that, she'll show you how to give each new arrival a pack of the basics to get them started. Then Pascale or Dixie will give them a medical exam and ask you to bring them over to Linda so she can vaccinate them. Once you have finished here and if you still have any energy left, perhaps you can help in the children's tent?'

Alice's stomach churned with anxiety. Help in the children's tent? She had no idea what that would involve, but Dante wouldn't have asked her if he hadn't thought it was something she could cope with.

Dante turned to Kadiga. 'Have you got anyone I should have a look at?'

'There is a family that Pascale is particularly worried about. She's with them now, but I know she would like a second opinion.'

'I'll go through,' Dante replied. 'I will see you later, Alice.'

The next couple of hours sped past. Alice did as she was asked, which was easy enough. Hassan squatted on the ground, never taking his eyes from her.

Once Kadiga noted the details of each new arrival, Alice made up a bundle for them. Coupons for their food ration, something to eat and drink from, a blanket. There was also a small pack consisting of plastic sheet, a pair of gloves, a disposable razor, a piece of string and a paper towel.

'We give this to all the pregnant women,' Kadiga said. 'This is what they need to have their babies. There is no room in the hospital tents for women who are having normal deliveries.' Kadiga also explained that the refugees who weren't ill were expected to make their own shelters from whatever they could find. The tents they had were already full and it was unlikely more would be arriving with the next convoy. Alice made a mental note to add more tents to her list of urgent supplies.

After the refugees had been seen by Pascale, a cheerful French woman in her forties, Alice took them across to Linda to be vaccinated. Despite the lack of shelter and the very basic facilities, it was a well-oiled system and Alice relaxed a little. All the time, little Hassan came with her.

When she'd taken her last patient to be vaccinated, Linda took her over to the children's ward. Linda indicated to Hassan to wait outside.

'This is it.' Linda opened the flap and Alice followed her in.

Alice was conscious of cots lined up against both sides, almost rammed against each other. Alice caught a glimpse of Dante's dark head as he bent over a patient. There were too many cots for Alice to count and from the look of the other children lined up outside, these were only the sickest of the patients. Some of the children had mothers sitting by the cots and some of the children were being held, but there were others who lay quietly crying with no one to cuddle them. Alice's heart ached when she saw them. How would it feel to be ill and have no loving arms to comfort you?

Alice was relieved to see that the money the organisation had sent was being put to good use but was it enough? It didn't seem to be—not nearly.

The tent was gloomy and they didn't appear to be using any of the hi-tech equipment Alice knew the charity had funded.

Linda caught her eye. 'We don't get electricity out here. We have a generator but it doesn't always work, so often we have to rely on good old basic skills.'

When Alice didn't say anything, Linda continued. 'Cholera is a big problem. Don't drink water from anything except the wells whatever you do. There are four at different points in the camp. There's a lake close to the periphery of the camp that the women use to wash—us too. You can swim there as long as you're careful not to let any of the water get in your mouth. I'll show you that when we get a free moment.'

Linda paused and looked around. 'I have to go to the adult tent to help Dixie. Could you find your way back to our tent? I'll come and get you later?'

Alice took a deep breath. She was exhausted and overwhelmed, but if the others were still working, so would she.

'No, that's okay. I'm fine, honestly. I'd rather keep going, if there's something for me to do.'

Linda laughed. 'There is always stuff to do. Could you help with the children while we vaccinate? The mothers will hold their own but there are a few kids here who have lost their parents and they could do with someone holding and comforting them.'

Alice was hardly aware of time passing as she threw herself into work. When Linda tapped her on the shoulder and said it was time to finish, she was surprised to find it was almost seven o'clock. The long line of patients had disappeared and the smell of cooking drifted on the evening air.

'C'mon. Let's get you fed,' Linda said.

'I don't know if I can keep my eyes open long enough to eat,' Alice replied.

'It gets easier. You've had a long day with an early start, but you have to make yourself eat, even when you don't want to. Everyone has to keep their strength up.'

Although every part of her body was aching to lie down and she was desperate to sleep, for the first time in a long time Alice felt she had achieved something.

'I'll just take Hassan back to his tent,' she said. 'He needs to have something to eat.'

After she'd left Hassan with his temporary family, Alice found her way back to the mess tent.

Dinner was some horrible white porridge and unrecognisable grey-looking meat that made Alice nauseous just to look at. Knowing that every morsel of food counted here, she forced herself to eat. Linda introduced her to the others who worked in the camp that she hadn't yet met. Hanuna, who was from Libya, and Dixie, who was American, were the other nurses Alice was sharing a tent with. Together with Linda, they covered the children's ward and the outpatient clinic, as well as dealing with any wounds, dressings or sick adults. Although they were friendly and cheerful, they all looked exhausted.

Needing some time to herself, Alice left the tent and found a rock to sit on a little distance from the main camp. She made herself comfortable and stared out at the horizon. The sun, a red globe in the darkening sky, turned the sand pink.

A footfall behind her made her whirl around. Dante was standing there looking fresh and alert as if he'd just got up from a long and refreshing sleep instead of having completed a twelve-hour shift. He hadn't been at dinner. When Alice had asked Linda where he was, she'd told her he was still on duty.

'How are you?' he asked. 'Linda says you did a good job today.' He crouched down next to her, balancing on the soles of his feet. 'I thought you might be in bed. You must be tired.'

'I couldn't sleep. I'm still too wound up.' She brushed a palm across her brow. 'It's an amazing place. Unbelievably beautiful. But unbelievably sad. Especially the children. Where are they all coming from? Where are they going?'

Dante followed her gaze out towards the silhouetted mountains. 'They come from all over. Some of them have been caught up in civil war. Some have no way of making a living where they are and the recent drought hasn't helped. They come in search of a better life but all they find is this. A lot save for years to pay someone to take them to Europe on boats. Mostly they get turned back.' His lips thinned 'Some don't even make it as far as Europe. The boats aren't exactly made for the rough seas.'

Alice shivered and wrapped her arms around herself.

'So many people without proper homes and so many children without parents. It's not right. What's going to happen to them?' Despite her best efforts her voice wobbled.

He looked at her sympathetically. 'We can't solve all the problems here, Alice. We can only do what we can, even if it doesn't seem much. We can't afford to get too involved.' His dark eyes were almost ebony. 'You can still go back. No one will think any less of you if you go. Being here is not for everyone.'

Alice stood up, brushing the sand off her trousers. 'I can cope,' she said quietly. 'I'm here now and I'm not going anywhere. Get used to it.' she smiled to take the bite from her words. 'We Granvilles don't give up easily.'

Something flickered behind his eyes. 'Good. We need you here.'

Her pulse skipped a beat. His words made her feel warm inside.

'I could do with a wash,' she said. 'Linda forgot to show me where the showers are.'

Dante grinned. 'I think shower is too grand a name for what we have here. There is a lake a little distance from the camp where the women wash their clothes. Some of us swim there. When we can't it is the bucket, I'm afraid. Throw it over your head or use a cloth.'

Alice was dismayed. She'd been longing for a shower. There was no way she could go to bed without a wash.

'I will get the water for you, if you like.' Dante suggested. 'There is always some being warmed on the campfire.'

'Just point me in the right direction and I'll get it myself.' Alice was determined that she wouldn't be asking for or receiving any special favours. Whatever everyone else did, she would do too.

Dante tipped her chin with his finger, forcing her to look him in the eyes. 'You have done a good job today. As much as anyone. And you had the long journey before. I will bring you the water, okay?'

A lump formed in her throat. She could almost bear his derision better than his kindness. She was too tired to argue, so she simply nodded. Now that the sun had disappeared the night was cold. She hadn't thought to bring a jacket. Dante held out his hand and helped her to her feet. His hand was warm, comforting. He put an arm around her shoulders and they started to walk back towards her tent.

'I will leave it outside, *cara. Buona notte.*'

As Alice stumbled towards her tent she could feel his eyes following her until she was safely inside.

CHAPTER SIX

THE next morning, after a sleepless night, Alice was up before the sun had risen but already the camp was stirring and the smells of cooking drifted across the camp. All staff meals were taken together in a communal tent. Breakfast was thin porridge or toast with coffee or tea.

If she hoped to see Dante before she started work she was disappointed. By the time she arrived at breakfast it was to see his disappearing back as he headed towards the children's tent. Linda asked her to go back to work in the reception area where all new arrivals were processed.

They came. Tired, sad and often ill. The children were the worst. The ones who had lost their parents. The ones with swollen bellies from lack of proper nutrition. As she'd done the day before, after she'd logged them in and given them their pack she took them to the clinic so they could be vaccinated and then passed them over to one of the other aid workers who found them a spot to set up some sort of shelter. Then she'd return and start the whole process all over again.

Midmorning, when she was dropping a patient off at the outpatient area, Linda called her over. 'Could you go to the children's tent and ask Dante to come when he's free? Tell him it's not an emergency but I have a patient I'm concerned about that I'd like him to see.'

Alice had been putting off going back to the children's tent. Out of it all, it was the children she found most difficult to cope with.

Inside the tent, it was almost eerily quiet. Babies lay looking up at the ceiling or stood up by the side of the cots staring in mystified silence at what was going on around them. About two-thirds of the children had a mother by the cot side, some of whom were breastfeeding while others were holding their children and singing or talking quietly to them.

But that left about six or seven children without anyone to look after them.

Dante was bending over a cot examining Samah, the child from the day before. When he noticed her, he straightened and spoke briefly to the child's mother before coming across to Alice.

'Hello. Have you come to help?'

Alice's heart was pounding but this time it wasn't because of Dante.

'I…' She faltered. How could she explain her reluctance to stay in the children's tent? She found the reality of the sick children almost too much to bear. She cleared her throat. 'Linda asked me to come and get you. She has a child in the clinic that needs a surgical opinion. Could you come? She says it can wait until you're finished here.'

'*Bene*. I just have to finish my rounds here first. I still have a couple of children to see.'

Alice stood at a safe distance, trying to ignore the outstretched arms of the toddlers without mothers. She watched as Dante examined the children. He was efficient but gentle, even managing to make some of the anxious mothers smile.

Alice kept flicking her eyes to the far side of the room. One toddler in particular was staring at her with wide brown eyes. It was the fact that the child made no gesture to be picked up, almost as if he or she had forgotten what it was like to be held, that disturbed her most.

She couldn't bear it any longer. It didn't matter what her personal feelings were. That child needed someone to pay it attention.

At the cot side she hunkered down to that she'd be at eye level with the child.

'Hello,' she said. She glanced at the chart. A single name: Bruno.

The child stared at her then he lifted his arms out to Alice.

She picked him up and he settled into her, his dark eyes never leaving hers for a second. A small hand reached up and touched her face. Alice's throat closed.

'I see you've met little Bruno,' Dante said softly. She hadn't heard him come up behind her.

'What happened to him? Why is he all alone?'

'His mother brought him here two weeks ago. Unfortunately there was nothing we could do for her.' Dante's eyes were bleak. 'Perhaps if she had managed to get here a day or two earlier, we might have saved her.'

'No other relatives? No one come to claim him?'

For the first time Alice noticed the lines around Dante's eyes. They seem to have deepened over the past twenty-four hours.

'No. Someone might still come. There are too many children here without parents. The other women do what they can with the ones who are well enough, but just getting through each day is hard enough without taking on responsibility for a sick child.'

Alice's mouth was dry. 'How sick?'

Dante crooked his finger and chucked Bruno under the chin. The child gave a small smile of recognition and stretched his arms out.

'I still hope we can make him better, but he's very weak.'

Dante lifted Bruno out of Alice's arms and into his own. 'How are you, little one?' Dante said softly. The child touched Dante on his mouth.

Dante hefted Bruno his arms. 'I think we have a wet-nappy situation going on. Could you change him,' he asked, 'while I finish my rounds? Hanuna and her assistant are both pretty busy.'

Change Bruno? Alice cast her eyes around the room, hoping for someone, anyone, that would get her out of this predicament. She had never changed a nappy in her life. Besides, didn't they have disposable ones? The soggy thing Bruno was wearing was made from cloth.

But how difficult could it be? And Dante was holding the child out, expecting her to take him. Gingerly, she accepted the toddler and as Dante turned away laid Bruno back down on his cot and unwrapped him. Free from the cooling restraints of his nappy, the little boy chortled and kicked his legs.

Now what? Where was she supposed to put the soiled nappy and find a clean one?

One of the mothers who had been watching the

scene with interest laid her sleeping baby back in the cot and walked over to Alice.

'You want me to do it?' she said.

'You speak English?' Alice was surprised.

The woman smiled. 'We learn it at high school. Many here speak a little bit if they went to school.'

Alice appreciated the offer of help but she wasn't going to give in at this first hurdle. She shook her head and smiled. 'Perhaps you could tell me where I find clean ones?'

The woman disappeared for a few minutes. While she was away, Alice leaned into the cot and touched Bruno's tiny hand. Little fingers curled around hers and big brown eyes looked into hers trustingly.

The mother came back with a set of clean nappies. Alice accepted one from her and tried to work out how she was supposed to form something that was square into something that would stay on the child. She folded it cross ways into a triangle. That didn't look right. It was much too big for a start. She tied various other combinations but they didn't look right either. Beads of sweat were forming on her forehead as she became increasingly flustered.

The mother who had given her the nappy turned to the other mothers and said something in Arabic. The women laughed. Soon Alice had four of them standing around the cot. At least she was providing some fun for them. She made several attempts to put the nappy on, but soon her hands were slippery with sweat. Why wouldn't the damn thing stay on?

By this time the laughter was causing more and more of the women to come across. They watched Alice's efforts speaking to one another and giggling. Then, to her mortification, Dante was there.

'Let me,' he said.

Alice stood back and there were more appreciative giggles from the women as, within seconds, Dante had Bruno changed and snugly wrapped up in his clean nappy.

Alice flushed with mortification. All she'd been asked to do was change a child and she hadn't even managed that. Dante was right. She was more of a hindrance than a help.

She blinked away tears that jagged behind her eyelids. She could learn. It was hardly surprising Dante knew what to do with children. He'd grown up in a huge family where there were always children. He had probably being changing nappies since he was a child himself.

Dante had just done this to humiliate her. To make a point. She would show him. She would show him that she could muck in and work as hard as anyone else. Even if it killed her.

'Okay, what else would you like me to do?'

'Why don't you ask Hanuna? I'm sure any help you can give with bathing and feeding would be appreciated.'

Hanuna gestured him over to one of the cots and Alice was on her own again.

Okay, so the nappy changing had been a bit of a disaster. But at least now she knew how to do it properly, she could do it again if needed. She hunted down Hanuna, who had finished consulting with Dante.

'I understand you need some help with bathing and feeding?'

The nurse flashed her a smile. 'It would be a help if you could feed some of the babies. Then if you're still willing, we could do with some help bathing the children. You'll need to get some water from the pump first.'

Hanuna found her a place to sit and showed her where to make up the feeds. 'Most of the babies are breastfed by their mothers. It's just the orphans who need to be given a bottle. We have five. Two are still on bottles, the other three are on soft food—a special high-protein supplement. The other mothers prepare that while they are doing it for their own children. Once you've bottle-fed the babies, go to the dining room and ask for the children's food. Okay?' Clearly impatient to get back to work, Hanuna pointed in the direction of two cots. 'If you start with the two babies there?'

Alice picked up the first baby. It was hard to tell but she thought the little girl was about eight months old. The child started crying, her mouth stretching wide with frustration or anger.

Alice took the baby with her while she fetched a bottle. She tested it on her wrist as Hanuna had shown her and sat down with the child cradled in the crook of her arm. She popped the teat in the baby's mouth and instantly the baby began to suck, staring up at Alice with intense brown eyes.

As the baby sucked contentedly, Alice glanced up and her breath caught in her throat. Dante was staring at her with the oddest expression. Her heart kicked against her ribs as their eyes locked. It was Alice who looked away first.

As soon as she finished feeding the child, she fed the next. Then she left them sleeping and set off to the kitchen to fetch the food for the others. She was feeling relieved and pleased. She wasn't useless after all. Already she was making a contribution and it felt good.

She fed the other three toddlers. Okay, this wasn't such a success. They squealed and wriggled and a large proportion of their food seemed to land on their bodies instead of their mouths. It was just as well they were still to have their baths. A couple of the watching mothers took pity on her and after feeding their own children came to help, giggling at Alice's efforts. Often she would look up to find Dante's eyes on hers as he moved around the room, examining the children and talking to the mothers. She had been aware of him leaving, probably to see the child Linda had wanted to talk to him about, and returning. It was as if her body had radar as far as he was concerned.

Once lunch was over, Alice headed out to the taps with a couple of buckets that she found by the door.

'Here, let me help.' Dante appeared by her side and held out his hand. He smiled down at her and her heart lurched again. It was the first time he had looked at her with anything except derision. In fact, could she be mistaken, or was that approval in his dark brown eyes?

Pretty pathetic if her feeble attempt at feeding was enough to make him revise his opinion of her. *If* he'd changed his opinion and that was far from certain.

'I can manage,' she said.

'I know you can.' He smiled at her through half-closed eyes. He took the bucket from her and as his hand brushed hers, a shock of electricity ran all the way down her spine to the tips of her toes. 'But you don't have to. I can do with some air for a few minutes.'

They walked together. 'You seem to be a hit with the women,' he said after a few moments.

'My attempts at child care make them laugh,' Alice said. 'At least I cheer them up, even if I'm slow and take far longer than everyone else.'

'Don't worry about taking your time, Alice,' he said. 'That's one thing everyone here has too much of. And the longer you take feeding the children, the longer they are being held. They don't get enough of that here.' His eyes darkened. 'We look after them physically as much as we can, but we just don't have time to look after their emotional needs. If all you do is cuddle and play with the children, that is enough.'

It seemed so little.

'Is there a crèche? A school?'

'Not yet. When we get time, we'll try and establish something. We have asked the main office to see if they can find a volunteer to do some teaching.'

An idea was beginning to form in Alice's head. She would have to think it through before she said anything.

They filled their buckets from a tap.

'What about heating it?'

'We take these buckets to those tents over there.' Dante pointed. 'A few of the women keep a fire going to heat the water for us. We give them this water in exchange for the heated water. It's a good system and the women are happy to help. Never ever be tempted to drink water that hasn't come from the well.'

Once they had swapped two of their buckets for hot water, they carried them back to the tent. Dante went back to work and one of the mothers helped Alice find a zinc bath. She took it the door and placed it in the sun. By this time Bruno had woken up and was regarding her solemnly over the bars of his cot. She decided to start with him.

The rest of the afternoon sped past. Finally the children were bathed and if not asleep were playing contentedly on the floor. Bruno seemed to have developed an attachment to her already. His brown eyes followed her everywhere.

When Alice had finished bathing and feeding the children she swung Bruno onto her hip and told the nurse she was taking him out for some fresh air. She hadn't fully explored the camp yet and she wanted to see if there was anywhere she could use for a small school.

Bruno was silent as she traipsed across the camp, but his big brown eyes kept looking around. It was the most animated Alice had seen him so far and she was even more convinced about her plan. These children needed stimulation.

As she weaved her way through the tents some of the women called out and waved. The little signs of recognition added to the glow she was feeling from being some help with the children.

It felt good to be needed. It felt good to be useful. Only now did it feel as if her life was making sense. Slowly, like sand filling a hole, that empty feeling she'd had all her life was leaving her. Why had it taken her so long to recognise that the life she was living was wrong for her? She had so much more to give.

It wasn't long before she found what she was looking for—a crumbling building made of mud with holes for windows. But at least it had a roof, even if that roof did have holes in it. It wasn't big, twenty feet long and ten feet wide at the most, but if she could use it, it would be perfect for a little school. She could persuade one of the mothers to look after the smaller children and perhaps one or two of the other women would help her teach the older ones. It wouldn't be much. A few words of English, some basic arithmetic, but anything that would keep the children occupied had to be good.

She would ask Linda or Dante when she saw

them at dinner, but she couldn't see why they would say no.

She was humming to herself when she returned Bruno to the children's tent.

CHAPTER SEVEN

ONE afternoon, a few days after she'd arrived, Alice decided to find the lake Dante and Linda had told her about. She needed to wash some clothes. More than ever, Hassan was a constant presence at her heels. He still didn't talk to her, but every now and again he would smile. His sister was still very poorly in the children's tent and although his mother was well again, she rarely left her younger child's side.

Alice had noticed the women coming from a little track on the far side of the camp, carrying their washing in baskets on their heads, and guessed that was where the lake had to be.

It was the first time she'd ever had to do her own laundry and she had to smile at how different her life was here at the camp. But she liked it. She liked it that everyone had to make do, that they all lived in similar conditions. No one was treated differently just because they had been born into a different social class or were rich. In many ways it was like being back in Italy that first time. She was ordinary Alice here too. This time everyone knew who she was, but didn't seem to care. Except Dante, of course.

On her way back from the lake, Hassan led her along a short cut through some bushes. Now, as she felt her hair, Alice knew why everyone stuck to the path in the clearing. Burrs from over-hanging bushes stuck to her hair like limpets. No matter how much she tried, she couldn't get them out.

She looked ridiculous. As if she was wearing some kind of maniacal hat. There was nothing for it. She would have to find a pair of scissors and chop them out. Oh, well, she had been thinking of cutting her hair ever since she had arrived. It was too long to be comfortable in this heat and difficult to keep clean.

Still tugging furiously at her hair, she popped into the dining hut, hoping to find someone who would help her cut it. Linda and Dante were sitting across from one another, chatting. Dante looked at Alice incredulously then grinned broadly.

'Is this a new kind of hairstyle from the catwalks?' he asked. He shook his head. 'Because, *cara,* I have to tell you, it's not a good look.'

'Very funny, Dante, I'm going to have to cut it. I don't suppose either of you have a pair of scissors on you, by any chance? Even better, you don't fancy cutting it for me, Linda?'

'Are you sure you want to? I envy your hair. It's so thick.' Linda drew a hand through her own short grey curls. 'If only I could turn the clock back.'

'I don't think there is any other way of getting rid of these burrs except by chopping them out. Besides, I've been planning to cut my hair since I arrived. I'm too hot and it gets in the way. It'll be a lot cooler and easier to manage if it is short.'

Linda shrugged. 'It's up to you, but I'm warning you, I'm no hairdresser. Hey, why don't you ask Dante? At least you know there's a good chance he won't lop an ear off.'

Dante looked at Alice and cocked his head to one side. 'I like your hair too. The burrs will come out if you have patience.'

Thank goodness it was hot and he wouldn't notice the extra heat that rose to her skin. Alice stood up. Dante cutting her hair was a ridiculous idea. She didn't want him that close.

'I can do it myself,' she said. 'I can use my nail scissors if necessary.'

Dante looked at her through slitted eyes, a smile playing on his lips. 'I will do it if you insist on cutting it.' He glanced at his watch. 'I have some time free now, if you like.'

Linda stood up and stretched. 'I'll leave you two to it, if that's okay. I have a couple of letters I want to write.'

'Really, Dante. I can manage by myself. There's a mirror in my tent,' Alice protested.

There was a gleam in his eye that she didn't like. He pulled her to her feet. 'Come on, or don't you trust me?'

Keeping hold of her hand, he guided her towards his tent.

Alice's heart was galloping. The thought of being alone with him made the blood rush to her head.

But he didn't take her into his tent. He left her standing outside while he retrieved a chair, a mirror and a pair of scissors from inside.

'Okay, you hold this and you can tell me when to stop cutting. First I think we need to wet it. It will be easier that way, no?'

He left her again and came back with a bucket of water. By this time a crowd of children had formed. They watched with the unfolding scene with big eyes. Alice smiled weakly.

Dante draped a towel across her shoulders.

'Bend forward.'

'Really Dante—' Alice started. But before she could finish he had bent her head and poured a bucket of water over her.

She gasped. Then strong fingers were massaging soap into her scalp. She told herself she would only make everything more farcical if she jumped up and tried to run away. As the shock of the cold water receded, Alice gave in to the sensations of his hands on her skin. His touch was playing havoc with her insides and she knew her body was covered in goose-bumps. She prayed Dante wouldn't notice.

'Just going to rinse,' Dante said.

Another cold shock of water. Some of the mothers had come to see what was causing all the excitement so that by the time Alice looked up, there was a crowd of about fifty watching.

Then he was rubbing her hair briskly with a towel.

'Okay, mirror.'

Obediently she held up the mirror. In its reflection she could see that Dante was smiling widely. At least every one else was having a good time.

His fingertips brushed the back of her neck as he lifted her hair and a delicious tingle ran down her spine. Then with one cut he snipped away her hair at the nape of her neck. There was a cry of regret and sympathy from the watching women.

Alice squeezed her eyes shut as bit by bit her hair fell around her.

'You can open your eyes now,' Dante spoke even-tually.

She peeked at the mirror. It wasn't *terrible*. Okay, it was spiky in places but on the whole she could live with it. Just as well. It wasn't as if she could stick the hair back on her head anyway.

Dante came around and crouched down in front of her.

'Not bad, though I say it myself. It shows your eyes.' He lowered his voice. 'Those beautiful green eyes.' His voice was a caress as he touched her mouth with his fingertip, turning her bones to marshmallow. Then abruptly he pulled his hand away and stood up.

The children clambered around him.

'Me next! Me next!'

Dante laughed and swung a little girl into the air. 'Sorry, guys, I have to get back to work.' And he walked off with four or five children clinging to his legs.

Alice shivered and tidied away the mess her

cut hair had left behind. This was going to be so much harder than she'd imagined. Seeing Dante every day, having him look at her, touch her. Why had she thought she could forget him?

CHAPTER EIGHT

EVENINGS were usually quiet, with most of the staff falling into bed shortly after dinner. That evening Linda told her that after supper they were having a campfire.

'It's not all work here. Everyone needs a chance to relax so when we can, we all get together and talk of work is strictly forbidden.'

After supper they all trooped to a small clearing where there had clearly been fires in the past. Dante and Costa arranged some stout logs around a pile of firewood and set light to the sticks. Within seconds the fire was burning fiercely.

The evenings in the desert were much cooler than the days, the cloudless skies sprinkled with stars. Alice held out her hands to the fire, glad of the warmth.

All the staff were there, except for Dixie, who

would stay on duty to keep an eye on the patients. Linda passed around mugs of sweet black tea.

'Don't you want to play us something, Dante?' Linda asked. 'I noticed you had your guitar with you.'

Smiling, Dante excused himself and returned a few minutes later with his guitar. He strummed a few notes and then began to sing in Italian. Alice and her colleagues listened in silence as Dante's low voice spilled into the night. That he could play the guitar and sing was another couple of facts to add to her growing list of things she hadn't known about him. How many more were there? Alice suspected that Dante was the kind of man she'd still be learning about for years to come.

The thought startled her. She had to remember that there wouldn't be more years for her and Dante. After this they would never see each other again. The pain that shot through her almost made her cry out.

She opened her eyes to find Dante looking directly at her as he sang.

For a moment the world stopped. Everything and everyone disappeared except Dante and herself. Alice's heart was hammering against her ribs so hard she could barely breathe.

She loved him. She could no longer pretend to herself. He was her heart, her soul, her world. Without him her life had no meaning. Only with him did her life make sense.

But was she prepared to give up everything she had discovered about herself, her new-found sense of who she was, to become part of his life? Not that he was going ask her.

She sighed and dropped her eyes. Why couldn't life be simple? Why couldn't she be herself and have Dante too? Was it too late? Could they find a way to be together that worked for them both? She didn't know. She was no longer the Alice who accepted what life gave her. She would fight for what she wanted and she wanted Dante. But first she needed to know whether Dante could love her.

There was a long silence as the last notes faded into the night.

'*Basta!* Enough!' Dante said. 'Costa, why don't you play something now?'

As Costa picked up the guitar and started singing a Greek song that had everyone clapping and tapping their feet, Dante slipped across to Alice.

Silently he held out his hand. Without thinking, she slipped her hand in his and let him pull her to her feet. Her heart was beating wildly as he led her away into the darkness. Neither of them said a word. There was nothing to be said.

Dante led her behind his tent and pulled her into his arms. Then his mouth found hers and they were kissing as if they'd never been apart.

She was gasping for breath when he finally pulled away. She couldn't speak, couldn't move. Just stare.

'Has any man ever kissed you like that? And did you kiss him back like you kissed me? When we made love, was it a lie too? Because, *cara*, I cannot believe that.' His eyes drilled into hers. Then he spun on his heel and walked away.

She stood there, watching his retreating back. She brought her fingers to her mouth. Had any man ever kissed her like that? No. Had she ever responded to anyone the way she had to Dante? Never.

She smiled. Dante might pretend to himself that didn't care about her, but she knew now he was fooling himself. All she had to do was make him realise the truth.

Dante put his hands behind his head and stared up at the ceiling. Costa was snoring gently but it wasn't that or the heat that was keeping Dante awake.

For some reason every time he closed his eyes, Alice's face would appear before him.

Damn. If he'd thought that bringing her here, reminding himself that she was a spoilt little rich girl whose idea of a hard life was having to walk to the shops, and that the daily reminder would get her out of his system, he'd been badly mistaken. Earlier, seeing her in the flickering light of the campfire, her hair cut short, her nose a little sunburned, she had reminded him of the Alice of Italy. He couldn't stop himself from leading her away from the others and kissing her, even if he had known that it was madness.

Feeling irritable, he turned on his side, his movement causing the camp bed to rock beneath him.

Every day that she was here she surprised him more. When he'd seen the shock and fear on her face when they'd arrived at the camp, he'd been certain that she would try and persuade her father to send a plane to evacuate her immediately. But she hadn't. Instead she'd buckled down and—he smiled at the memory—even if her nappy changing, feeding and bathing skills left a great deal to be desired, she had stubbornly refused to be defeated. The staff had nothing but praise for the way she was always asking to help and never complained. The mothers and the children liked her. She was easy with them. Gentle and considerate.

He turned over onto his other side and thumped his thin pillow.

These last few days she had done everything that was asked of her and more. Wherever he looked she was there, taking care of the children—she had improved hugely over the last few days—and now managed bathing and feeding almost like a pro. When she wasn't doing that, she was helping the women carry water or firewood or playing with the children. And when she wasn't doing that, she was at the reception tent, helping to register the refugees. Whenever she wasn't working he'd catch sight of her walking around the camp with Bruno on her hip and a gaggle of giggling children, including Hassan, running behind.

Knowing that he wouldn't be able to get back to sleep, he tossed the bedclothes aside and slipped out of bed, careful not to make a sound. He slept in scrub bottoms at night, knowing he could be called at any time. Although dawn was still an hour away, it was already warming up and the camp was beginning to stir. He needed to cool down.

Grabbing a towel from the hook near his bed, he headed towards the lake. If he was quick he'd have time for a swim before the women came down to wash their clothes.

He loved this time of day. When it was quiet, apart from the chirping of the crickets, and he had some time to think. Not that thinking was doing him much good.

He padded his way down to the lake. As he'd hoped, it was deserted. He yanked off his scrubs and dived into the water, gasping as the cold hit him.

He swam for thirty minutes until he was sure the nervous energy that had been building up over the last few days had diminished. Now surely he'd be able to work without being distracted by images of Alice.

There was a sound from the bank of the lake and he turned to find Alice standing staring at him.

So much for trying to get her out of his head.

Alice was rigid as she watched Dante power his way through the water. In the silvery light of the dying moon he was barely visible, but she would know that dark head anywhere. He must have had the same idea about coming for a swim. Maybe he'd been here before and they'd just missed each other? Swimming was a better way of getting clean than the awkward shower arrangement where you pulled a bucket of cold water over your head behind a makeshift screen, but Alice had learned that she had to get up really early if she didn't want an audience. Clearly this morning she hadn't got up early enough.

She was about to turn and go back when he called out her name. He was treading water.

'Don't go.' His voice was urgent. 'I mean, you don't have to leave because of me.' He gestured with his hand. 'It's a big lake. There's plenty room for both of us.' His teeth flashed in the light of the moon.

Alice hesitated. He was right. And she did want her swim. It was the best way she knew of getting set up for the day. It might be a big lake, but nevertheless the image of her and Dante in it together, naked, was playing tricks with her head and heart, not to say libido.

'Turn around first,' she said.

He smiled again but did as she asked.

Quickly she pulled her T-shirt over her head and slipped out of her shorts. Leaving on her underwear, she waded in, shivering as the cool water encased her. Frightened in case he turned around, she forced her head under the water and came back up gasping for air.

Dante had lied about keeping his distance. Still treading water, he had swum over to the where she had emerged. The sun was beginning to lighten the sky and there was just enough light for Alice to see his eyes. He was so close she could see his dilated pupils.

The water suddenly felt several degrees warmer.

He reached out and touched her shoulder. She could feel every one of his individual fingertips on her skin and she knew it wasn't the cool water that was giving her goose-bumps.

'You've caught the sun,' he said. His voice was low and his eyes looked dazed.

Her heart was doing weird flip-flops again.

She turned on her stomach and started to swim away from him.

When she heard the sound of Dante getting out of the water, it took every ounce of her willpower not to turn her head to look at him until she was sure it was safe to do so. He had pulled on his scrub trousers and was rubbing his hair with a towel.

She was getting cold. If she stayed where she was any longer, she would freeze. It was ridiculous to care that Dante was still standing there. Why was he anyway?

She waded out, stooped to pick up the towel she had left by the side of the lake and wrapped it around her body. Dante hadn't moved a muscle.

'Don't tell me you're checking I make it back to camp in one piece.' She smiled. Her words came out all breathy, not the way she wanted them to at all.

He stepped towards her, his mouth set in a grim line. He touched her hair. 'It suits you,' he said. 'You look like Alice again.'

He dropped his hand and ran the back of his

hand down the side of her face. Then without another word he spun on his heel and walked away, leaving Alice feeling as if the sun had gone behind a cloud.

A few days later, Alice was up just as the sky was lightening. The clinic wasn't due to start for another couple of hours. Although she loved being at the camp, there was never a moment when she could be on her own. While that was good in one way, she had no time to think, and today she felt the need to be on her own, even if for a little while.

She took her drawing pad with her, the one luxury she had allowed herself, and crept out of her tent, careful not to wake her sleeping colleagues.

Alice headed off in the opposite direction from the lake. She wanted to sketch the scene as the sun rose over the mountains.

A bird called in the distance and the crickets chirped from the undergrowth. The air was perfectly still and it was cool. When the sun rose it would get blisteringly hot.

She found a flat rock to perch on and as the sun turned the sky lavender, she began to sketch. Since the ill-fated class she had taken in Italy she had continued to draw. She was still no better than she had been but she didn't care. It was the one activity where she could lose herself.

She pulled out a folded piece of paper. It was the drawing she had done of Dante that day back in Italy that seemed so long ago. She studied the picture and smiled. Although it was terrible, she had never been able to bring herself to throw it away. It reminded her too much of a time when she'd been truly happy.

Placing it down on the rock next to her, she picked up her pencil. She sketched fast, drawing the mountains and the multicoloured clothes that the women had left drying on the rocks. She was so intent on what she was doing she didn't hear anyone approach until a shadow fell across her notebook.

She looked up to find a man she didn't recognise standing in front of her.

Alice scrambled to her feet. 'What is it?' she asked. Her heart skipped a beat. It was lonely out here. If she needed to call for help, would anyone even hear her?

The man leaned across and touched her arm. He was speaking rapidly in a language she couldn't understand and seemed frustrated with her lack of comprehension.

He grabbed her by the arm and started pulling her. Now she was truly afraid.

Dante stepped into the clearing. His mouth was set in a grim line, his eyes narrowed against the sunlight. He said a few words to the man that Alice couldn't understand. After a few moments' conversation, Dante broke into a wide smile.

'His name is Matak. He says he has heard you want to make a school. He says he knows how to build one and will help you.'

Immediately Alice felt ashamed. 'Tell him I would like that and that I'm sorry for not understanding.'

'He says he will get some more people and see what can be done.'

The man melted into the bushes.

Shaken, Alice sat back down on the rock. What was Dante doing there anyway?

'Were you following me?'

Dante folded his arms. 'I was working out next to my tent when I saw you come this way. A short while later I saw him follow you.'

'And you've been watching me all this time?'

'I wanted to make sure you were okay. He was watching you too. I couldn't be sure what his intentions were but I couldn't leave until I knew you were safe.'

'Since when is my safety any of your concern?'

'I would have done the same for any woman in this camp,' he said. 'Although we try we can't stop or vet everyone who comes here. A lot of the people who find their way here are desperate. They have no money, no home, no life. Desperate people do desperate things. As it happens, he meant you no harm and wanted to help, but you can never be too careful.'

The anger leaked out of Alice, to be replaced with disappointment. She didn't want him to see her as simply a woman he had to watch out for the way he watched out for them all.

'Thank you,' she said softly. She picked up her pad from the ground. 'I'd better get back.'

Dante stepped forward and lifted the paper she had left on the rock and it fell open in his hands. He studied it for a moment and Alice's heart almost stopped. What an idiot he would think her, bringing that silly sketch of him all the way out here.

He grinned, folded the paper and passed it back to her. He said something in Italian that she couldn't understand. She wasn't sure she wanted to know.

He placed a hand on her shoulder. 'Are you really going to try and build a school? Aren't you doing enough?'

The kindness in his voice brought an unexpected ache to her throat. Although she loved it here, it was so different from anything she had ever experienced. She'd tried to hide it, but she was tired and often the cases they dealt with upset her. How could she have been so isolated, so wrapped up in her pampered life that she had been unaware of what life was like for so many of the people she shared the planet with?

'*Cara*, what is it? Why are you crying?'

She hadn't been aware of the tears running down her cheeks. Mortified, she brushed them away while turning her back on him, knowing that if she didn't she wouldn't be able to stop herself throwing herself into his arms and sobbing her heart out.

Dante swung her around so she was facing him. 'It is okay to be sad,' he said. 'It shows you are human.'

Alice managed a weak smile. 'Was there any doubt?'

'Yes,' he said, softly 'Once, I did wonder if you had a heart.'

'And now?' Her pulse was still pounding but she knew it was no longer because she was frightened.

'You are different. You've changed.'

'Oh, Dante. I don't think I've changed at all. I think, here, I am the person I was always meant to be.'

They stared at each other and for a moment she thought Dante was going to kiss her again. She swayed slightly towards him but to her dismay, he stepped back, gave a little shake of his head and took her by the elbow.

'Don't come here by yourself again. Understand?'

Embarrassment gave way to anger. 'I'll do as I please, Dante.' She shook his arm away. 'You have no right to tell me what to do outside the camp. You said I've changed, and I have. I'm perfectly able to look after myself. The last thing I need is for you to look out for me. The sooner you realise that, the better.'

She stomped off back to the camp. However she felt about Dante, she would not let him treat her like some kind of inferior just because she was a woman. If there was one thing she wanted right now, it was for him to realise for once and for all that she was someone who could manage her own life.

CHAPTER NINE

'Is there any chance I could use the building on the far side of the camp as a school?' Alice asked Linda at breakfast. 'It would be a much easier solution than trying to build one.'

Dante, who was sitting next to Linda, looked up from his coffee.

Linda shook her head. 'Sorry, we need it. We're going to use it for another ward as soon as we get some sort of roof on it. I've been meaning to organise it for a few weeks now, but there never seems to be the time.' She took a sip of tea. 'The school is a good idea, but you'd have to construct a shelter or something to hold classes yourself, I'm afraid.'

Alice smiled. 'As it happens, I met one of the men down at the lake earlier. He'd heard from some of the women that I was thinking of making a school and he offered to help me build one. He said others would help too.'

Dante frowned at Linda. 'Why didn't you tell me you were waiting for a roof on the building? Costa and I could do it with some help from the men in the camp.'

'I didn't ask you, Dante, because you hardly have a moment to eat and sleep without me putting more on your shoulders.'

Dante placed his hand on top of Linda's. 'I can always find the time.'

'I could help,' Alice offered. 'If Matak shows me how. We could fix the roof as well as building a school.'

Dante opened his mouth as if he were about to protest but seemed to change his mind.

'Why not?' he said with a smile. 'Nothing you do surprises me any more.'

As soon as she'd finished her breakfast Alice went in search of Matak.

True to his word, he had gathered a group of men and women ready to help with whatever was required to create a space for the children to learn. One of the women who spoke English explained to Alice what Matak wanted them to do.

'We take mud and mix it with water. Matak has made some frames for the bricks. We pour the mud into them and pound it with our hands.' Alice watched as Matak demonstrated. 'After that we put the bricks out of the frames and leave them in the sun to dry. When we have enough bricks, we will make a wall. Then we will use wood to make the rest.'

Okay, Alice thought. That sounded easy enough. But by the time she had made three bricks she was already exhausted and the sweat was making her T-shirt cling to her skin. She eyed her bricks uneasily. They looked misshapen and not at all like the ones the others had made.

She straightened and eased the kinks from her aching back. In the time she had been working they'd been joined by several others from the camp. Women, men and even children ranging from age seven to seventeen. Hassan was there as usual and appeared to have elected himself as her personal helper. He kept feeding her the wet mud, plodding determinedly between mud pile and her work station. If he could do it, so could she. Once more she bent to her task, only stopping when she felt a shadow fall across her brick-making station.

She looked up and squinted. Dante was framed against the sun. He looked like some fallen angel and Alice's heart raced.

'*Dio*, what are you doing now?'

'Building a school. As I told you I was going to.' Her knees were so stiff Dante had to help her to her feet.

'I didn't think you were going to be actually building it. Don't you ever stop?'

'We need a school. Matak said he knows how to build one. So that's what we're doing. I can hardly stand by and just watch while everyone else works, can I?'

Dante reached out and took her hand in his. 'Your knuckles are bleeding.'

Alice looked at her bleeding hand in surprise. Intent on her task, she hadn't noticed. He was right. But it was her nails that horrified her most. They were split and cracked and covered with mud. They would never be the same again. But it no longer mattered. None of who she'd been in her past life did any more. Nails would grow again. Children had only one chance at a future. As she looked around, she saw that between them all, they had made almost a hundred bricks.

Grinning, Dante whipped off his shirt and with a few words to the watching crowd he offered to take Hassan's shovel. When the little boy shook his head, and hid his shovel protectively behind his back, Dante smiled and picked up a different one.

'Don't you have somewhere else you need to be?' Alice asked as she knelt back down at her station.

'The nurses know where to look for me if they need me. It seems to me, though, you could do with some help here.'

They worked together as the sun continued to beat down. The women and the men sang as they mixed mud and pounded their bricks.

Dante smiled to himself as he watched Alice leave the brick-making, only to return a short while later carrying a load of wood on her back. Her hair was mussed up and she had a smear of dirt across her nose, but she had never looked more beautiful to him. He had been badly mistaken thinking she was some spoilt princess. The woman who worked here and had won the admiration of the camp was the same woman that had driven him crazy with longing back in Italy.

Alice threw the wood to the ground with an explosion of breath.

'I'll never complain about the gym again,' she muttered. But she smiled at him and it was as if the sun had come from behind a cloud. Her eyes were sparkling like the sun on water.

At that moment a nurse came to fetch Dante and he was kept occupied with patients for the rest of the afternoon. When he returned to the makeshift building site, planning to put in another couple of hours on the school, he was alarmed to find Alice still there. This time she was on top of the old building that Linda wanted to use as an extra ward. Balancing precariously on the top, she was helping Matak and several others bind bunches of wood together for the roof.

He wanted her down. She must be exhausted and tiredness would make her careless. She could slip at any time and if she did, she could break a bone, or worse. Even if she didn't, the others were used to physical work in the heat of the sun, but Alice wasn't.

Not wanting to call out to her in case he distracted her, he swung himself onto the roof and felt his way across the narrow walls until he was by her side.

'Alice,' he said softly. 'I think it's time to finish for the day.'

The smile she gave him made his head spin. 'Isn't it great? We have to wait a day or two for the bricks to dry so we thought we'd start on this roof. Everyone's been helping.'

Although her face was pale with fatigue, her eyes were dancing. 'I think Matak sneakily threw away a few of my bricks, but he says I'm getting better.'

She looked so sexy standing there with her mud-splattered hands on her hips that had they been alone and on the ground, he knew he wouldn't have been able to stop kissing her until she was breathless.

'Alice, as one of the doctors at the camp, I'm insisting that you stop for the night,' Dante said, more roughly than he'd intended. He needed to get her safely on the ground.

He could tell by the determined set of her mouth that she wasn't going to agree so he played his ace. 'The nurses say Bruno won't settle. They think he's looking for you.'

Alice stopped what she was doing. 'Bruno? He's not crying is he?' She brushed her hands on her mud-splattered trousers. 'I'll go to him straight away.'

Dante had to steel himself to watch as Alice made her way along the narrow wall before climbing down. *Dio*, if anything happened to her he'd...

The thought stopped him in his tracks. God, he loved her. He knew that now. More than he'd thought it was possible to love a woman. He loved her as he had never loved anyone before or would again. But the realisation gave him no pleasure. Despite everything, despite the fact she had shown everyone she was able to face whatever life in the camp threw at her, a future between them was impossible. He could never give this woman the life she was used to. A life she was soon going back to.

CHAPTER TEN

THE days continued to speed past. Every morning Alice went to the children's tent and helped bathe and feed the orphans. After that she would spend a couple of hours in the registration tent, making sure the records were up to date.

Whenever she had a free moment she would scoop Bruno up from his cot and play with him. Every day she was getting more attached to the small child and she didn't know how she was going to be able to leave him when the time came for her to go home. He wasn't putting on as much weight as she would have hoped, but he seemed brighter and smiled much more often. When she entered the children's tent his eyes would seek her out and he would lift his arms towards her, waiting for her to lift him. She would talk to him as she bathed and fed him, delighting in making him smile. Then she would help with the other children. If there was time, she'd grab something to eat, usually on the run, before rushing off to open her small school, which they had managed to complete in under a week.

It was her favourite part of the day. She would gather the children, around twenty of them, with ages ranging from four to fifteen, and teach them English and basic arithmetic.

They listened avidly, lapping up anything Alice could teach them, and if one of the younger children became fractious then the older ones would pick up the child and soothe it so the lesson could continue.

She was happy and for the first in her life truly fulfilled. She dreaded the thought of leaving, and not just because of Bruno.

But would she have to? Her father had written to tell Alice that he was getting married again, so there was no longer any reason for her to go back. At last she was free to live her own life. Do what she wanted to do rather than what a sense of duty and responsibility dictated. Maybe she could come back to the camp or do something else to help. It was an exciting thought and she promised herself that she would speak to Linda about it when she got the chance.

Even more than going back to her old life, she hated the thought of Dante leaving. In two weeks he'd be gone and she'd never see him again and the realisation was tearing her apart. Since the episode down at the lake he had seemed to go out of his way to avoid her, although sometimes she would catch him looking at her as if she puzzled him.

This morning one of the children, a little girl, was unusually quiet. Alice had been keeping an eye on her since lessons had started a couple of hours earlier, and instead of the child's usual attentive demeanour she was sitting listlessly, her eyes almost closed.

Alarmed, Alice crossed over to her and felt her forehead. She was a little hotter than she would have expected, but that was all. She looked closer. The little girl's eyes were red, but that could have been caused by the incessant dust. Then she saw it. Small purplish spots on her skin. Something definitely wasn't right.

Leaving one of the mothers in charge of the rest of the children, she scooped the child into her arms and ran towards the sick children's tent. Somehow she knew that whatever was wrong with the child, it wasn't good.

Dante looked up as she burst into the tent, still carrying the child. The look on her face must have told him that something was badly wrong and he rushed across to Alice.

'What is it?' he asked urgently. He looked down at the child and he must have seen what Alice had. He lifted the child out of her arms and carried the unprotesting form over to an examination coach.

Alice stood by, hardly daring to breathe as Dante examined the little girl.

'It's measles, isn't it?' Alice asked. Whenever she had free time, she had taken to going to the mess tent and browsing through the medical reference textbooks. She had seen a photograph of a child whose skin looked just like this.

Dante nodded. 'How did you know?'

'I saw a photograph in one of the textbooks in the mess. Is it bad?' She also knew from the same reference books that while measles was a fairly benign illness most of the time, it could sometimes have devastating results, leaving a child deaf, or infertile, or even dead. And that was healthy children. Not these desperately underweight scraps.

'I don't know. But it's good, very good that you spotted the symptoms straight away. If we've caught it early enough, there is no reason at all to think that she won't recover.' He squeezed her shoulder. 'Well done, Alice. You may well have saved her life.'

But the little girl was only the start. One by one the children fell ill.

If they hadn't been malnourished to begin with, the illness wouldn't have been so severe. At least now that the brick house had a roof, it could be utilised as a makeshift ward. Within days they had ten sick children and no one wanted to hazard a guess how many more there would be before the disease ran its course.

The school was suspended and Alice went to see Dante.

'Tell me what to do to help,' she said.

Dante glanced up from the small child he was treating. His eyes were shadowed with fatigue.

'If you can help nurse the children it will be a help. Linda and the other nurses still have their normal duties and patients to look after and they are all overstretched already.' He rubbed the back of his neck. 'It will be rough,' he said. 'Perhaps you'd be better off doing something else.'

Her expression must have told him he was wasting his breath and he gave her a resigned smile.

'Okay. We can do with all the help we can get. What I need you to do is to make sure that all the children are kept as cool as possible. Go around the cots and take a fresh bowl and bathe each child. If you can, get them to drink something at the same time. When you've finished, start all over again.' He placed his hand on her shoulder and looked into her eyes. 'We might not be able to save everyone. You do know that, Alice?' His voice was gentle but he couldn't disguise the naked pain in his eyes. She knew how much every loss meant to him. Each one was his childhood friend all over again.

Unable to trust herself to speak, she nodded her head.

She started at the first cot, where a little girl with grey skin and shrunken cheeks was looking at her with empty, despairing eyes. Icy tendrils wrapped themselves around Alice's heart. It was Samah, Hassan's sister. She had been improving the last time Alice had seen her. But that had been before she had caught measles.

'I'm going to make you feel better, sweetie,' Alice whispered, knowing that if the child couldn't understand her words she might at least get comfort from the tone of her voice.

The next forty-eight hours passed in a haze. Alice barely left the little ward except to catch a few hours' sleep and neither did Dante. Sometimes she wondered if he rested at all.

As she bathed the sick children and took them into her lap to feed them small sips of water she watched Dante. He moved from cot to cot, checking drips and listening to little chests. Almost as soon as one child got better and was transferred to the non-contagious ward, another would take its place.

During a break, when she had seen to every child, she left the tent and fetched a mug of strong coffee for Dante as well as some food. He was poring over charts when she returned.

'Here, drink this,' she ordered. When he shook his head, she placed the mug and plate in front of him and folded her arms.

'I'm not going anywhere until you finish eating and drinking what I've brought you,' she said firmly. 'For once…' she wagged a finger at him '…you are going to listen to me.'

Dante picked up the mug of coffee. 'I always knew you liked to give orders,' he said, but his smile was genuine.

'How long do you think before the epidemic burns itself out?' she asked.

'I'm not sure. The incubation period is one to two weeks. The first case was three days ago. I think we should be past the worst of it soon.'

'Thank God.' So far they hadn't lost any children, although Hassan's sister was still giving them cause for concern. Because she had only just arrived in the camp, her body hadn't had a chance to recover from the lack of nourishment she'd experienced over the previous months.

Dante took a distracted bite of his sandwich and stood.

'I need to check on Samah,' he said, tossing his half-eaten sandwich on the table.

Alice followed him to the cot. She watched as Dante adjusted the drip and listened to the child's chest.

When he looked up his eyes were bleak. 'I don't think she's going to make it.'

'No!' Alice's throat ached. 'Can't you do anything?' she asked. 'There *must* be something. You can't let her die!'

Very gently Dante placed his hand under her chin and tipped Alice's head until she was forced to look into his eyes. Her tears prevented her from seeing the expression in his.

'I want you to go and get one of the nurses. Can you do that?'

Alice didn't want to leave, but she could hardly refuse to get help. Perhaps there was still a chance they could do something to save the little girl.

Dante was carefully removing the drip from Samah's veins. Alice could see that the area where the drip had been was swollen. Her heart in her throat, she watched as Dante lifted Samah into his arms.

'Go, Alice,' he said roughly. 'And don't come back until later. Go and see Bruno. Spend time with him. Then get some sleep.'

As she turned to go the last thing she saw was Dante holding Samah in his arms, whispering softly to her.

Tears blinding her, Alice ran. She made her way to her favourite rock by the side of the lake, put her head in her arms and howled. She couldn't bear it. It was too cruel. All too much for her.

What about little Hassan? How would he cope with the loss of his sister? She would go to him, but not now. Not until she had got some control.

She didn't know how long she'd been there, but she was aware of him before she saw him. He crouched down beside her and pulled her into his arms. He didn't have to tell her that Samah was gone and she couldn't stop herself from sobbing again.

'Shh, *amore*, shh,' he whispered into her hair. 'It's okay.'

'It is not okay,' she mumbled into his chest, uncaring that the front of his shirt was soaked with her tears. 'Dante, it is *not* okay. None of this is.'

He moved around until he was crouching in front of her. He held onto her shoulders. 'I would give anything for that not to happen,' he said, 'but we're not miracle workers, no matter how much we wish we were. We have to think about the ones we save, not the ones we lose.'

He lifted her chin with his finger. Even in the dim light of the moon she could see the naked pain in his eyes. 'Are you going to be okay?' he asked.

Alice took a deep, shuddering breath. 'I'm selfish, thinking about myself. But, Dante, if it's the last thing I do, I'm going to make sure that more people know what is really happening here. I can't do much, God, I can't do anything to save a life out here, but I have to do something to change things. Children shouldn't be left to live and die on their own.'

He smiled at her. 'That's my girl. Use your anger to do something that will make a difference. But you should know that you have—even in the short time you have been here. You help with the children, Bruno has someone to love him, Hassan adores you, you have your school. You amaze me.'

'Do I?'

He stood and pulled her to her feet. 'Yes. You make me proud. You should be proud of yourself.'

He wrapped his arms around her and started leading her back towards the camp.

CHAPTER ELEVEN

TOWARDS the end of her time at the camp, Alice went into the children's tent to fetch Bruno for their usual walk around the camp. She saw little of Hassan these days. He clung to his mother's side as if he was frightened that she too would disappear. Thankfully the measles epidemic had ebbed, with poor Samah being the only fatality. Although they all mourned the loss of the little girl, Alice knew enough to realise that it could have been a lot worse if it hadn't been for the skill of the doctors and nurses. She had played her part too. A small one, it was true, but no less important.

This morning, however, there was no smile for her from Bruno, no raising of small arms to be lifted. Instead he lay in his cot, looking up at her with listless eyes.

Alarmed, Alice bent over him and touched his cheek with a fingertip. His skin was hot, too hot to be attributed to the heat of the day.

Her heart lurched in her chest. Something wasn't right. She cast frantic eyes around the room until she located Dante. He was deep in conversation with the nurses. Alice scurried over to them.

'What's wrong with Bruno?' she asked, uncaring that she was interrupting the conversation. 'He's hot and barely seems to recognise me.'

The nurses looked at her with sympathetic eyes. It was no secret how attached Alice was to the little boy and no secret how badly she had taken the death of Samah.

Dante took her by the elbow and led her away to the only quiet corner of the room.

'I am sorry. Bruno has taken a turn for the worse, I'm afraid. He's stopped eating and unless we can get him to take something to drink, we'll have to put him on a drip. Even then…' he touched her gently on the shoulder 'I don't know if he'll make it.'

'What do you mean, not make it?' Alice's throat was dry. Of course she knew what he was saying but she needed to hear him say the words.

'You should prepare yourself, *cara*. Unless Bruno's condition starts to improve dramatically within the next twenty-four hours, I think he is going to die.'

'Die?' She still couldn't—wouldn't—believe what she was hearing. She shivered and wrapped her arms around herself. 'He can't die, Dante. You can't let him. *I* won't let him. We cannot let another child die. If he needs more care than we can provide here I'll get my father to arrange an air evacuation to take him to hospital somewhere where he can be looked after.' She wasn't aware that she was crying until she tasted the salt of her tears.

Dante lifted his hand and with his thumb gently wiped her cheeks. 'There's no time to arrange that, Alice. It will take at least a day to organise an air ambulance. Besides, there is nothing a different hospital can do for him that we can't do here.'

She was not going to let Bruno die. It was simply not going to happen.

She breathed deeply and squared her shoulders. 'What do we do?'

'His temperature needs to be kept under control. That means a cool bath every couple of hours. He needs to be given fluids as well. As often as he'll take them. That is all we can do.'

'Right then. I'd better make a start.' She whirled around but Dante grabbed her by the elbow again. He tipped her chin, forcing her to look into his eyes.

'He will probably die anyway, *amore*. You need to know that.'

Alice wasn't going to accept that.

'Not if I have anything to do with it.'

She left Dante and returned to Bruno's cot side. Bending over the cot, she whispered, 'I'm here, sweetie. And I'm going to make sure you're okay. First I have to get stuff to give you a bath. That will make you feel better. Then I'm going to feed you, and you are going to take it.' She didn't know what, if anything, the toddler understood of what she was saying but her intent must have been obvious. Bruno smiled trustingly at her and lifted a languid hand. Her heart ached as the little fingers wrapped themselves around hers.

The next hours were a blur. Alice bathed Bruno before lifting him into her lap. It took ages for her to coax each mouthful of fluid between his parched lips, but she wasn't going to give up. Every so often one of the nurses would come and check the little boy's pulse and blood pressure. Alice refused to catch their eyes but she could tell from their sympathetic eyes that they were convinced she was fighting a losing battle. She sang softly to Bruno, willing him to live with every fibre of her being.

She was barely aware of Dante until he crouched beside her and placed a hand on her shoulder. 'You need to rest.' Dante's voice was soft.

'I'm not leaving him. Not until I'm sure he's okay. Don't even think of trying to make me.'

Dante smiled, although his eyes remained bleak.

'I'm finished here for the moment. I'll hold him while you go and get something to eat.'

But Alice shook her head. How to tell him that she was scared that if she left Bruno even for a moment he might give up the fight. For some reason she couldn't explain she believed the little boy was holding on because of her. But she was glad Dante was there. She drew strength from his presence.

'In that case, I will go and get us both something to eat,' Dante said. 'I'll be back soon.'

It seemed like seconds before Dante was back with a plate piled high with food. One look at it made Alice's stomach heave. How could she even think of eating when Bruno was so ill? Alice shook her head at Dante.

'Try and eat something,' he said. 'Give me the little one to hold for a while.'

Reluctantly Alice handed Bruno across to Dante. She couldn't eat but she knew she should drink something. And she needed to go to the bathroom. She knew Dante wouldn't let anything happen to Bruno in the few minutes she'd be away.

When she came back Dante was leaning back in his chair with Bruno asleep in his arms. Alice's heart stuttered. The child looked so small. So fragile against Dante's broad chest. In another life that might have been their child he was holding.

'See?' He smiled at her. 'Bruno is sleeping. It is good.'

Not wanting to disturb Bruno, Alice pulled up a chair next to Dante. Night had fallen and the nurses had dimmed the lights. Most of the other children were sleeping with their mothers beside them on a mat. It felt as if it was only the three of them awake, only the three of them in the world.

'It isn't good to get too attached to the children here,' Dante said. 'It will hurt you in the end.'

'How can you say that?' Alice whispered back. 'How can you do what you do and not care?'

'I didn't say I didn't care.' Dante paused. 'All I am saying is that it is better not to care too much.'

Like I cared about you. Like I care about you.

Like you cared about your friend. You are a liar, Dante. But she kept the words to herself.

'I think it is better to care too much than not to care at all,' Alice said. 'Even if it hurts so much you think you'll die from the pain of it.'

Dante looked at her intently. 'And have you? Ever cared too much?' he asked.

'Yes, I have. And I have lost people I loved, but I know now that loving them and losing them was better than not loving them at all.'

'Your mother?' Dante guessed.

'Yes, my mother. She left me and Dad when I was five.' It was the first time she had spoken of her mother to anyone. Her father had always refused to talk about his ex-wife and Alice had always wondered how her mother could have simply upped and left.

As a five-year-old she had never been able to understand why her mother had been there one day and not the next. She had waited for her to come back, but she never had, until eventually Alice had stopped waiting for her to come back.

Did Bruno, even though he was so much

younger, wonder why his mother had left him? He was far too young to understand that it hadn't been her choice. Unlike Alice's mother. In time, as she'd got older and read about her mother in the society pages of the newspapers, Alice had learned that her mother had left her husband and child to lead a new, unencumbered life with a younger, even richer and better-connected man than her father.

'I couldn't understand why my mother didn't live with us the way other people's mothers did. Whenever I asked my father he would brush me off with some comment about my mother being different from other women. I don't think he ever got over the way she left. It was why I had to stay near him. Apart from me, he didn't have anyone else.'

Dante took her hand and threaded her fingers through his.

'Oh, Mother would send me presents, extravagant presents, but all I really wanted was her. She'd also promise to come and see me the next time she was in London, but that only happened once. When I was seven. She came like this beautiful vision from a film and only stayed for an hour or so. I begged her to take me with her, just for a holiday, but she only smiled and said that her new husband wasn't very good with children. That was her second husband. Apparently her third didn't like children either because she never did take me to live with her.'

'I cannot understand how any woman could leave her children. In Italy this is unheard of.' There was no mistaking the anger in Dante's voice. 'I feel sorry for the child you must have been. At least you had your father.'

It was on the tip of her tongue to explain that her father hadn't spent much more time with her. He had been too busy making his fortune. At least she'd always known her father loved her. In return she had stayed with him knowing he depended on her. Only now that he was getting married again did she feel able to follow her own heart. If only that could include Dante too.

'In Italy the man likes to spend time with his

children. It is not a duty for us. It is a pleasure and a privilege.'

'Even if it means spending less time on your motorbike?' Alice teased.

Dante smiled back. 'We can do it all. We work, we eat, we are with the children. It is how it should be, no?'

'What about the woman? Can she do it all?'

Dante looked puzzled. 'She has her home, her children, her friends and her husband. If she wants to work too, that is also okay.' Dante studied her. 'She should do what makes her happy.'

'What if she doesn't know what makes her happy? Or what if she knows but can't have it? What then?'

Dante looked puzzled. 'If we are talking about you, and I think we are, then you already have what you want, *sì*?'

Alice felt her temper rise. 'You think you know me, Dante, but you don't. You don't know the first thing about me. You certainly don't know what I want now. If you did...' She was prevented from finishing her sentence when Bruno stirred and gave a faint cry. Instantly she was on her feet and removed him from Dante's arms.

'What is it? What's wrong, Dante?'

'Hey, hey. It's okay. It is a good sign, I think. The quiet baby is the sickest one. If he is crying it could mean he is beginning to get better.' Dante unwrapped his stethoscope from around his neck and pressed it to Bruno's tiny chest. Alice held her breath. Please, God, she prayed silently. Let him get better.

Her heart skipped a beat when Dante looked up. His serious expression had cleared and he smiled at her. 'He is breathing better now.'

Relief coursed through Alice's veins. Before she knew it she was crying. Deep, sobbing gulps that shook her body. She was crying for Bruno, for all the children in the camp, the adults too. For herself and for her own lost childhood, but most of all she was crying for what could never be.

Somehow she was in Dante's arms with Bruno caught between them and Dante was murmuring words to her that she didn't understand. She didn't care. Just this once she wanted to rest in the cocoon of his embrace. To feel as if she belonged somewhere, as if she was the most precious thing in the world to someone. Even if the feeling was imaginary.

Eventually her sobs subsided and she pulled away.

'I must look terrible.' She sniffed. 'I don't know why I'm crying. I seem to do it all the time these days. Even when I'm happy.'

'You have never looked more beautiful.' There was something in Dante's voice Alice couldn't identify. 'But you mustn't get your hopes too high. Not yet. Bruno could seem to make an improvement for a short while, but his condition could still deteriorate.'

'We're not going to let that happen to him, are we?' Alice replied.

Alice stayed with Bruno through the night and, apart from going to get them coffee to keep them both awake, Dante stayed too. Together they bathed Bruno and fed him little sips of water.

Whenever the child slept, which was with increasing frequency and increasingly deeper, Dante and Alice talked. By unspoken mutual agreement they kept away from what had happened between them in Italy, sharing instead the small details of their lives. Alice told Dante how she had packed a bag stuffed with toys and books and left one night on a mission to find her mother. Fortunately, although it hadn't seemed so at the time, her absence had been discovered before she was halfway along the drive and she had been brought home.

Dante had laughed and told her how as a boy he had been released from his house with a chunk of bread and half a cheese and instructed to check up on the animals in the fields. He had stayed out for the whole day, happily making up adventures that usually involved him vanquishing some mythical enemy. Whenever he'd got thirsty he had found a stream and curled an oak leaf into a curl to make a cup.

As the sun began to rise in the sky, Dante turned to Alice. 'What are you going to do when you leave here?' he asked. 'Are you going back to being Lady Alice?'

Alice looked down at Bruno. The heat had left his skin and his breathing was deep and rhythmical. Every now and again his eyes would flicker open and he would stare into hers. Satisfied that she was still there, he would fall asleep again.

'No,' she said. 'I'm never going back to my old life. I know for sure that I need more. That's something I've learned since being here. Up until now I have let others tell me what to do, but I'm not going to do it any more. I want to carry on doing voluntary work with the camps. It's one thing being able to look after the immediate needs of the people here, but what about the long term? They need education, proper homes, stability. I'm going to find out what I can do to make that happen. I'm going to try and make some people's dreams come true.'

Dante eyed her speculatively. 'I have no doubt you will,' he said quietly.

CHAPTER TWELVE

BRUNO improved a little every day and soon Alice was able to return to her routine. Bruno wasn't fit enough for her to take him with her, but she visited him whenever she had a chance. Every time he ate a full meal or giggled as he played, Alice's heart soared. But then, when she remembered that she would be leaving in a few days' time and would be leaving him for good, she thought her heart would break.

'What will happen to him?' she asked Linda.

'He will probably be placed in one of the orphanages,' Linda said. 'He'll be well looked after.

'Do you think I could adopt him? Take him back to the UK with me?'

Linda looked at her with regret. 'I'm sorry, Alice, that won't be possible. One day his family might come looking for him. He is bound to have aunties and uncles, maybe a grandmother out there who might be looking for him. No one will agree to let him be adopted if there's the slightest chance he has a family that wants him.'

'But what kind of life will he have here? If I adopt him I can give him everything. The best of education, love. Especially love.'

Linda touched her on the hand. 'We will keep track of him for you and you can come back and visit him. It's not really fair to take him away from his family if they want him. No matter how much you would give him.' She lowered her voice. 'I know how much you love him, Alice, but maybe you can do something for all the orphaned children instead of just one? Think about it.'

Alice did. She had been thinking of nothing else over the last couple of weeks. To start with she would speak to her father about funding a children's home. Somewhere with a small school attached. If he wouldn't fund it, she would. She was due to inherit a sum of money on her next birthday and she could think of nothing she wanted to do with her money except put it to good use. A smile on one little face was worth more than a hundred designer gowns. And as for parties and dances, who cared? She'd rather spend an evening around the campfire with this group of people. No, she wouldn't miss her old life one little bit. She needed to go back so that she could speak to her father, but then she'd come back to Africa. Alice knew she had found her purpose and she was happy. As happy as she could be with the prospect of leaving Bruno and Dante.

Dante watched as Alice sat outside her makeshift school with her children. As usual Bruno was never far away. She couldn't have looked more different from the woman he had seen the night of the fundraising dinner. Her golden hair, now cropped short, framed her pixie face, which was lightly tanned by the sun. She was wearing a T-shirt and cotton trousers that she had rolled up to her knees. Whenever he saw her around the camp she was surrounded by children. They followed her everywhere. When she wasn't at her little school, she was in the children's tent, helping to feed and bathe the children. Any spare time she had she spent with the orphans, often just holding them, singing in her soft, husky voice. And she helped the women too. Going with them to forage for firewood or accompanying them to the well for water. He had seen her once trying to balance a pot on her head and although she had failed miserably, she had made the women with her laugh.

Alice looked up as he passed by and their eyes locked. Her eyes were no longer sad, and she seemed to glow from an inner happiness. The camp would miss her when she was gone. *Dio*, he would miss her too.

Later that day she came to find him in the children's tent. She looked unsurprised to find him holding Bruno. He had got into the habit of taking a child with him on his rounds. It was unconventional, but Alice had shown him that physical contact with the children was as important as any medicine he could give them. Alice hadn't been the only one to learn something from her time here.

'Linda asked me to come and get you.' Alice said. 'She has something she want to discuss with us.'

'Okay, let's go and see what she wants,' Dante said, placing a sleeping Bruno back in his cot. 'I'm finished here for the time being.'

Alice followed him out of the tent and across to the other side of the camp.

But it seemed as if it wasn't a patient Linda wanted to see him about.

'We're running low on supplies,' Linda told them as she tidied up. 'Normally I'd contact Luigi to ask him to bring more, but I've been thinking that it would be a good idea for the pair of you to go instead.'

Dante and Alice both started protesting, but Linda cut them off with an impervious wave of her hand.

'The pair of you need time out. You've both been working day and night, with the measles epidemic and everything. Everyone else has had a day off except you two.'

'It's out of the question,' Dante insisted. 'There is too much for Pascale to do on her own.'

'But she won't be on her own. Lydia is returning from leave. She's arriving later today and is planning to start straight away. She's fully rested and you aren't.'

Alice had learned enough about Linda to know that when she made up her mind about something, she wouldn't be thwarted. And from the expression on Dante's face he knew it too.

'Besides,' Linda continued, 'we do need more supplies and it's always useful to have a doctor to check that they've given us the right stuff. So no more arguments. You're both going.'

Alice slid a glance in Dante's direction. His expression was hooded so she couldn't read how he felt about spending time with her on their own.

Dante still looked unconvinced. But then he seemed to realise Linda wouldn't be swayed. He smiled ruefully. 'I can see you have made up your mind. And Alice does need a break.'

'Good,' Linda said with a relieved grin. 'In that case, you should go tomorrow morning. I'll make sure Costa has the truck fuelled and ready for you.'

Dante turned to Alice. 'We should leave at daybreak. We can camp on the way if you like. I know a good place near shelter and water. It'll be better than staying in the city. Don't take too much. We will need all the space for supplies.' He grinned at her and Alice knew he was thinking back to the day she had arrived back in Italy. She wouldn't be surprised if even the tips of her ears were red with embarrassment. But she had come a long way since then.

At daybreak the next morning Dante was already waiting for her when she emerged from her tent. She had done as he asked and her rucksack was practically empty, apart from a change of underwear.

He eyed her rucksack warily then, seeing it was practically empty, grinned.

'What no hairdryer? No books?'

She hit him on the arm and he pretended to

reel from the blow, even though she had barely touched him.

'Be gentle,' he teased. 'You've developed muscles since you've been here.'

Alice laughed. In this frame of mind he reminded her once more of the easygoing, mischievous Dante she had first met and she was secretly delighted. Although she loved him in every mood, it was good to see him relaxed. Could it be that he was looking forward to being alone with her? Her pulse rate quickened. This was possibly the last opportunity she would have to find out whether he loved her enough to want to be with her. She couldn't bear to think about how she would feel if he didn't.

The sky was burnished gold as they set off. Being in the truck brought back memories of their trip out here. It was incredible to think it had only been three weeks. It felt like a lifetime.

Dante explained that they would drive for the morning before stopping for lunch. After a few more hours in the truck they would reach the spot where he planned to set up camp for the night.

'Unless you'd rather keep going until we come to a town?' he asked, looking uncertain for the first time.

'Camping sounds perfect,' Alice reassured him. Every moment she had left with him was too precious to share with others.

As they bumped along the uneven track they passed more people making their way towards the camp, but soon even they disappeared until the only sign of life was a lonely buzzard hovering in the cloudless sky. The folding sands of the desert stretched into the distance where the mountains rose up from the sand like ghosts.

They stopped to stretch their legs and have something to eat but almost immediately they were on their way again. It was late afternoon before the track came to an end and Dante brought the truck to a halt.

'The place I had in mind is just down in that valley,' he said, pointing to a green-rimmed dip between two hills. 'A stream runs through it, so we can have water for coffee and to cool off.' For the first time, tension filled the air between them.

Alice jumped out of the truck and helped Dante load a few supplies into their rucksacks.

As they walked they chatted about the camp. It was the one safe subject of conversation.

'You love what you do here, don't you?' Alice said. 'But what about Italy? Your home and your family? Your job?'

'I'll always go back to Italy. That is where my family is. But one day?' He shrugged. 'Who knows? I like it that life is full of surprises.' He glanced at her. 'At least some of the time.'

'What is that supposed to mean?'

'Just what I say.' He stopped and looked at her, hard. 'You have surprised me, *cara*. I thought you wouldn't cope with life in the camp, that you'd be begging your father to take you away, but I was wrong. I don't think anyone in the camp works harder than you.'

Pleasure at his praise washed over Alice. At least she knew now that he saw that she wasn't the spoilt heiress he'd assumed her to be. She knew he liked her and approved of her, but she wanted more—much more.

When they found Dante's preferred spot they set about gathering wood for a campfire. As they unpacked their food for their meal, Alice had to smile. This time she had come prepared with plenty of food from the camp. What had she been thinking the last time? No wonder he had thought her spoilt and incapable of coping with the conditions in the camp. At least he had admitted he had changed his opinion.

She shivered with anticipation. Tonight they would be alone for the first time since the night they'd spent together in Italy.

As the sun continued to sink in the sky, turning the sand dunes rose, Alice became increasingly nervous. Would he try to kiss her again? It was what she wanted. This could be the last chance she had to be with Dante. Her last chance to find out if he still cared for her and if they could have a future together.

Dante set out their sleeping bags. Out here

there was no need to worry about mosquitoes and they'd be able to sleep under the stars.

Alice looked at the stream longingly. 'Do you think it's safe to wash in it?' she asked Dante.

'Probably. It comes from the top of the mountain where it's fast flowing, but it's probably safer to boil it first for our coffee.'

As he set about making a fire to heat the water, the air between them grew thick with tension. Once the water had boiled Dante set it aside to cool while they ate the food they had brought with them.

'We should get some sleep,' Dante said eventually. 'The water will be cool enough if you prefer to use that to wash. Leave some for me, if you can.'

It was now or never.

Did it really matter if she made a fool of herself? At least she would have one last night with him to remember.

Slowly she unbuttoned her blouse and slipped it off along with her trousers. Standing in her bra and panties, she dipped her cloth into the water and squeezed it out over her breasts. She knew what she was doing.

Dante was watching her through half-closed eyes.

She took her time washing herself, although she left her underwear on. 'Your turn now,' she told him.

She crossed over to him and pulled him to his feet. Then she ran her hands up the sides of his torso and pulled off his T-shirt. She dipped her hands in the water and, taking the sliver of soap she had brought with her, worked up some lather and rubbed her hands across his chest, exploring the ridges of his muscled chest, following the lines of his scar with her fingertips.

He made a sound deep in his throat and his eyes darkened. 'Be careful, *cara*. Do not start what you can't finish.' But he didn't pull away from her.

Her heart was in her mouth. 'I don't want to stop,' she said. 'I want you.'

His hands were behind her and he undid the clasp of her bra. As her breasts sprang free, he moaned and lowered his head to drop kisses on each breast.

She couldn't stop now, even if she wanted to. And she didn't. As if they had a mind of their own, her fingers found the button of his jeans. He shifted away from her just long enough to let her slide his jeans over his hips. Her breath caught in her throat at the sight of his naked body.

He hooked his fingers in her panties and with one swift movement she too was naked. Her body was throbbing and she could no longer think straight. All she knew was that she had been waiting for this moment since the last time they had made love, possibly all her life.

He placed his hands under her bottom and lifted her up onto his waist. She wrapped her legs around him, wanting to feel every inch of his skin next to hers. Wanting him. Needing him.

She clung to him as he bent his head and kissed her. Then suddenly he was inside her and, his hands still on her hips, he was moving her against him. She flung her head back to allow him access to her throat and her breasts and she was kissing him too, tasting his skin with her tongue, loving him, needing him, knowing that finally she had come home.

Later they lay wrapped in each other's arms on top of Dante's sleeping bag, which he had unzipped to make a blanket for them. Night had fallen and the stars peppered the sky like silver bullets.

'I love you, Dante,' she whispered into the night. 'I have loved you almost from the day I met you.'

He pulled her closer and ran a hand through her hair. 'I love you too. I will never stop as long as I breathe.'

Happiness spread through Alice. She hadn't been mistaken. He did love her.

'But it is no use now, is it?' he said gently. 'You and I can never be together. There is no future for us. What we have away from here isn't real.'

Alice felt as if someone had wrapped her heart in ice. She sat up and crossed her arms across her breasts.

'Why not?'

'Because loving each other isn't enough, is it?' He shifted his body until he was sitting behind her with his long legs on either side of her. He wrapped his arms around her, pulling her into the cocoon of his arms. 'Because, *amore*, I can't give you the life you are used to. I am not a rich man, not by your father's standards.'

'But I have money. We can use that.'

His hands were caressing her throat, his touch as light as a child's kiss. She caught his hand in hers and kissed his fingertips. His groaned against her hair.

'I can't, *cara*. Don't you understand? I am Italian. We have to support our families ourselves. It is the way for us. A man who doesn't support his family is only half a man.'

'I'll give it away. To the charity. I don't need it. All I need is you.'

He brushed the top of her head with his lips. 'I know you think you can live with me now, but soon you will come to resent me.'

'Dante, that's ridiculous! We don't live in the nineteenth century any more. What's yours is mine and what's mine is yours. That is part of loving someone. And haven't I shown you that I don't need money? I've never had so little financially yet I've never felt richer. Why let your stubborn male pride get in the way of our happiness? If you do, you can't really love me.' Now she was getting angry. She gripped his arms and pulled herself upright. 'I'm prepared to come and live with you in Italy if necessary. Live in a strange country away from everything and everybody I know. Yet you won't make any concessions at all.' Her throat was tight. 'You decide. I love you, Dante. Enough to give up everything for you. The question is do you love me enough?'

'All I know, *amore,* is that I need you, right now.'

And then once more she was in his arms and he was kissing her as if his life depended on it.

CHAPTER THIRTEEN

THE next day they repacked their belongings and set off once more. After making love they had lain in each other's arms without saying anything. What more was there to say? Alice had given him her heart and still it wasn't enough. But he'd said he loved her. Why, then, was he so determined to not to give their relationship a chance? He was putting his pride before their happiness so perhaps he didn't love her as much as he said. She shook her head. That wasn't right. She knew with a deep unshakeable certainty that his love for her was real and strong.

If Africa had taught her one thing, it was that she was stubborn too. If Dante was prepared to give up on them, she wasn't. But how to persuade him?

They made their way back up the hill to the truck, both wrapped in their own thoughts.

Back in the truck they soon left the mountains behind and were crossing the open desert. Although she didn't mean to, Alice felt her eyes close. She had tossed and turned last night, unable to stop thinking.

She was jerked out of her dreamless sleep by a violent bang. Dante was struggling with the steering-wheel as the truck veered from side to side. Out of the darkness a cluster of boulders rose in front of them. Dante swore under his breath as he struggled to avoid them but it was no use. The sound of screeching metal rent the air as they hit the rocks.

Alice couldn't tell how long she'd been unconscious. She moved her limbs tentatively. Hot stabs of pain were shooting through her foot, but otherwise she seemed all right. But what about Dante? The silence in the truck terrified her.

She turned her head. He was still in the driver's

seat with his eyes closed. There was a frightening amount of blood coming from a wound in his head.

Alice reached over to feel for his pulse, the way she'd been shown at the camp. Please, God, let him be all right. A sob escaped from her throat as she felt his pulse beating beneath her fingertips. He was alive. For now. There was no way she could tell how badly he had banged his head or what other injuries he might have. All she knew was that if he died, her life wouldn't be worth living.

'Dante, please open your eyes.' He was only dimly aware of Alice bending over him, her green eyes wide with terror. He tried to move to gather her to him, but something was pinning his arm. He groaned. *Dio*, he felt terrible.

'What happened?' he managed. His mouth was dry.

'We crashed. Into some rocks. I don't know how. I was asleep,'

It came back in a rush. The tyre exploding,

the truck veering across the road. The rocks and knowing there was nothing he could do to avoid them. After that...nothing.

'Are you okay? Are you hurt?' He tried to shift in his seat so he could see her better but Alice gently pressed him back into his seat. 'Don't move. Isn't that what you told me when Sofia and her grandmother were in that accident? Stay still until we know how badly you're hurt.'

She had covered him with her jacket and placed something else behind his head. Tears were rolling down her cheeks. He would have given anything to pull her into his arms and comfort her.

'How long have I been out?' he asked.

'About twenty minutes. How are you feeling? Your face is cut but I think it's stopped bleeding. I found some bandages in the rucksack.'

As Dante tried to raise his arm to check the wound to his forehead, he had to bite down hard to stop himself yelling out. The pain in his shoulder told him he had damaged it. Something was either broken or dislocated. Using the fingers of his left hand, he felt his forehead. The wound wasn't as bad as it probably looked to Alice. Head wounds had a habit of bleeding copiously. He shook his head, trying to clear it, and winced. As far as he could tell, that was the sum of his injuries. He needed to find out how badly damaged the truck was. He had to take stock of their situation, decide what to do.

'I have to get out and have a look at the damage. But you'll have to open the door for me. I can't use my right arm.'

Alice ran around to his side and opened the door. He tried to brush away her fears with a smile. 'Hey, remember I survived a bike crash at speed so a little bump on the head and a sore shoulder is nothing.' But he could see by the way she puckered her brow that his ruse hadn't worked.

As soon as he saw the truck from the outside, he knew that any thoughts of using it to get back to camp were out of the question. The front tyre must have exploded, which had caused the accident. They could have tried to drive on the rim of the wheel if it hadn't been for the fact that the front of the truck was twisted almost beyond recognition. The look he shared with Alice told him she already knew that the vehicle wouldn't be going anywhere.

'I've checked our water.' Alice said. 'We have two litres. We also have a little food and some antibiotics and bandages.'

Dante was impressed by the calm way she'd assessed their situation.

He felt his shoulder tentatively and his fingers came away sticky with blood.

'I should dress that for you.' Alice said, digging around in the rucksack.

He sat, hoping his head would clear, but even through the fug in his head he was conscious of her cool fingers on his skin. First she placed a dressing over the wound, then she fashioned a sling out of one of the other bandages. When she'd finished she stood back and surveyed her work with satisfaction. 'Not too shabby, though I say it myself.'

She was right. Although blood was still seeping through the bandage, it would stop eventually. The frustration was in not being able to use his arm.

'How long do you think it'll be before someone comes looking for us?'

Too long. That was the problem. Linda and the rest weren't expecting them back until later on tomorrow at the earliest. It would be a couple of days before they would come looking for them. Dante didn't know if they could survive until then. He looked around. All he could see for miles was desert. No shelter. No sign of humans. Only a buzzard circling overhead.

'They could come any time. As long as we stay here, they'll find us eventually.' There was nothing to be gained in alarming Alice.

Alice nodded. He could tell from the determined set of her mouth that she would do everything she could to survive.

'*Cara...*' He touched her on the cheek. 'I'm so sorry for getting you into this mess.'

She smiled slightly. 'Just as long as you stay alive long enough to get me out of it, you're forgiven. Anyway, it wasn't as if you caused the tyre to blow.'

They agreed to ration themselves to a sip of water every half an hour. The sun was high in the sky, beating down on them. They moved away from the truck to the shelter of a nearby baobab tree.

Alice leaned against the thick trunk. Although it was still hot, at least the shade offered some relief from the heat of the sun.

'You know, Dante, if one of us had a mobile, I could call my father and get him to send help. You wouldn't say no to using my money then, would you?'

'But that is different,' he protested. 'I would do anything, use anyone or anything, to get you out of this.'

Alice smiled slightly. 'But you would give me up because of your male pride?' She shifted slightly so she could see into his eyes. 'There is a chance we won't make it, right?'

He opened his mouth to protest but she brought a finger to his lips. 'Please, Dante, I think I've earned the right to the truth, don't you? You have to accept that I am a grown woman and treat me like one. If you don't, there's every chance I'll beat you about the head.'

He tried to summon a smile, but couldn't. Didn't she know how serious their situation was? Then he realised that of course she did and he admired her more than ever. 'Maybe you should leave me here and go on without me,' he said. 'You can take the water and you'll make better time on your own. All you have to do is stay on the road.'

'Leave you, Dante?' She raised her eyebrows at him. 'Damn it, darling man, when will you realise I am never going to leave you again?'

There was no answer to that. Alice was constantly surprising him. A different woman might have wept and railed when they found themselves in the position Alice found herself now. But she hadn't. She had taken care of him and with quiet determination thrown in her lot with his. If he'd doubted that she was the woman he'd first fallen in love with, he had no such doubts now. If anything, he loved her more. She had dealt with everything he had thrown at her and although it hadn't been his intention to make them face death together, she was dealing with that in the same quiet way he had come to love. And, *Dio*, he loved her. More than he had thought it was possible to love a woman. Even with her eyes rimmed red from the dust she was the most beautiful woman he had ever seen. More beautiful to him than the Alice decked out in all her finery and jewels. A woman he would be proud to call his wife.

She was right. He was letting his male pride get in the way of the only person who would ever make him happy. If he didn't have Alice, he didn't want anyone. But what if she came to resent him after time? What then? What if it was after they had children? Would she leave and take them with her?

He shook his head and the sudden movement made his shoulder ache. There was no answer to his problem. Not one he could live with. If they lived.

'What is it, Dante?' her voice was anxious. She must have noticed him wincing.

'It's nothing. A little pain. That is all.' It was the truth. The pain in his shoulder was nothing compared to the one in his soul.

The day wore on with the sun beating down relentlessly. Alice kept a watchful eye on Dante, certain that his shoulder was more badly injured than he had let on. They shared the remaining water, taking fewer and fewer sips as the level in the bottle continued to fall.

'Maybe I *should* go for help?' Alice suggested. 'You could stay here and if anyone comes you could pick me up. I'll stay on the road.'

'No,' Dante said sharply. 'You were right. We have to stay with the truck. At least here we have a little shelter from the sun. And it's much easier to see than one person on a road.' He smiled tightly. 'I know you're much fitter than you used to be, *cara*, but no one can last in this heat. No matter how fit or how brave.'

'You think I'm brave?' Alice didn't try to conceal her incredulity. 'I thought you believed me to be a spoilt rich girl?'

He had the grace to look sheepish. 'I was angry with you when I said that.' He hesitated. 'I thought that was why you wouldn't stay in Italy when I asked you.' He twisted around so he could see her face clearly. 'I know now that you are not and I'm not sure any more that you ever were.'

'You were right in one sense.' It was time for them to be honest with each other. It was possible that they could die. Dante didn't need to say it but Alice was damned if she was going to die without telling him the truth. All of it. 'When you asked me to stay longer, part of me wanted to. But I was scared. Scared to leave my life in the UK behind. Scared that if I stayed even a night longer with you then I would never be able to leave. And I didn't want to tell you who I was, about the life I lead. I was too ashamed.'

When Dante opened his mouth to say something, she stopped his lips with her fingertip. 'Will you let me finish?' When he nodded she continued, 'You just wanted to extend the time we had together, without promises. What then? I would still have had to leave some time and it already hurt to go when I did. Think of your life back then, Dante. You did exactly as you pleased. Working at the hospital, going on your bike, seeing your friends, giving any spare money to your family. We both knew that there was no future for our relationship. I was falling in love with you, but I could never walk away from my life. And you? I didn't know how you felt, but you weren't making any promises, were you?' She took a deep breath. She had to be totally honest with him. 'I was wrong too. I should have been honest with you right from the start.'

Dante used his good arm to pull her close. 'I loved Natalia. I cannot pretend that I didn't. When she left me because I wasn't rich enough for her, I vowed to myself I would never love another woman. But you made me love you.'

'Hey, I said you've to let me finish.'

'You have changed,' Dante said, but there was a small smile on his lips.

'I haven't changed all that much, Dante, except perhaps, as you say, I'm braver. That's what I'm trying to say. Even if I had stayed longer and we had fallen in love, my love for you wouldn't have made the empty feeling I had inside go away, not for ever. Can you understand that?'

'And now? What do you feel inside now?'

'As if I'm whole. I'm ready now to love, to lead my own life, and I want that life to have you in it. I love you. More than I thought it possible to love someone. Without you my life will still have no meaning.'

He traced her lips with a finger letting his touch trail down to her collar bone. *Amore mio,* I feel the same—don't you know that?'

A surge of happiness almost took her breath away.

'But we can never be,' he finished, and her heart plummeted.

'Why not?'

'You are rich and a man must provide for his woman. It is how it is.'

Alice hid a smile. Dragging Dante into the twenty-first century wasn't going to be easy, but one thing she had learned recently was that she liked a challenge.

'Oh, Dante. I am no longer as rich as I thought I was going to be. My new stepmother is pregnant and the scans have shown that it's a boy.'

Dante frowned. 'I don't understand.'

'Before this, I stood to inherit. But now that there is to be a son, my father wants to leave the bulk of his fortune to his new child. And he has my full agreement.'

'You don't mind? But it isn't fair.'

'We're not so different in the UK as you are in Italy. It is better that the family home goes to one child. This way, the house stays intact in the family.'

'So you're not quite the spoilt little rich girl any more?' Dante asked. There was a hopeful ring to his voice that made her smile again.

Alice laughed. 'Not quite. However, my father

plans to leave me a generous sum, apart from the allowance I receive now, so I'll still be very well off. It will be enough to build a children's home, maybe two, maybe eventually more, here in Africa. I know it will take time to get the permissions, but for once I'm going to let my father help me. I've never really known what I wanted to do with my life. Until now it has been all mapped out. Finally I've found something I need to do. I want to work full time with refugees, helping with the long-term solutions. What we do at the camp is great, but it only deals with the immediate problems. The people here need decent places to stay, schools, children's homes. People to lobby for them in other countries.' She smiled wryly. 'I fully intend to use all the contacts I've built up as Lady Alice to make sure the people here are not forgotten.'

'And what about marriage? Children? Aren't they important?'

'Yes. I want children. One day. First I have to do this. Can you understand?'

Dante rested his chin on the top of her head.

'After we argued, I went to the villa to look for you. When I saw it, the size of it, the swimming pool, the helicopter landing place, I began to suspect you hadn't been honest with me, that you weren't who you said you were. The housekeeper wouldn't give me your address, but I was going to come to England and try and find you. Then I got your note. You made it clear that I wasn't to look for you. When I saw you in England, I was almost sure it couldn't be you. I wanted it not to be. But despite the clothes I would recognise you anywhere. I knew then why you left and I cursed myself and you. You most of all for not being the woman I thought you were. I was angry, *cara*, I wouldn't deny it, but I couldn't stop thinking about you.'

Alice was listening intently.

'Then when you asked to come to Africa— okay, not asked—when you told me you were coming, I didn't know what your motives were. I couldn't see you here. I thought you wouldn't last a minute. When I suggested you go on the hike, I didn't think you would manage and that you'd be on the next plane home. And as for me? I thought seeing who you truly were would get you out of my head.'

Alice smiled into his chest.

'But I proved you wrong.'

'I didn't know whether to be pleased or disappointed. All I knew was that I wasn't ready to say goodbye again.'

His hand was in her hair and the feel of his fingertips on her scalp was sending goose-bumps down her arms. 'But I should have sent you back. We wouldn't be in this mess now.'

'I wouldn't have gone. None of this...' she waved her hand in the direction of the desert '...is your fault. These last few weeks have been the happiest of my life.'

He kissed the top of her head. 'Seeing you here, the way you were with the women and children, just made me love you more. I love you, *amore*, more than I can say. You are my heart, my home, my love.' He smiled grimly and sighed. What use was his pride without her? She was prepared to give up everything for him and he would rather have her with all the difficulties that might entail than live a second of his life without her. If they lived through this.

'You are right, *amore*. I have let my pride rule my heart. I know I couldn't love you if you weren't who you are. It will be difficult for me, to have you as my wife, knowing that you will want to lead an independent life too, but I will learn to do it. If you will have me. Will you, Alice Granville, marry this stubborn Italian man?'

Alice swivelled in his arms until she was looking into his eyes. She needed to be sure, but what she saw in his face must have convinced her.

'Just try and stop me.' This time their kiss was different. There was passion and love but most of all tenderness.

After a while Alice spoke again. 'What now?'

'You mean when we get out of here? I'm going to make everything all right between us. We will marry and have babies and live together for the rest of our lives.'

'And my plans? What about them?'

'I can see that I was wrong, and selfish. A year

ago, I couldn't have lived with a woman who wasn't content to look after me and our children. In that you were right. Now I couldn't live with a woman who wasn't you. If you want to spend your life working with aid agencies, then I must let you. We will have our babies when you are ready.'

'Let me?' Alice teased. She knew it would take time for him to change.

'Support you, I mean.' He smiled. 'It won't be easy, *cara*, I can't promise you that sometimes I won't resent the fact that I am not the sole provider, but I'll do my best.'

'We'll be together? Wherever that is?

Alice knew what she was asking. For Dante to leave his country and his family to live and work in a strange country was a big ask.

'*Cara*, wherever you are is where I want to be.'

They talked, sharing their hopes and dreams as the night wore on. As day was breaking they saw in the distance a plume of dust.

'It's a car or a truck.' Alice said. 'Dante, we're going to be all right!'

He wrapped her in his arms. '*Amore mio*, we are going to be more than all right. We are going to be perfect.'

EPILOGUE

IT WAS two years exactly since the day they had first met, and two months since the night they had spent in the desert not knowing if they would live to see this day. Dante's shoulder had been surprisingly quick to heal and the rest of the time had been taken up in a whirlwind of wedding arrangements and organising for the orphanages they were planning to build.

Dante had handed in his notice at the hospital and had been assured that when he was ready to return there would be a job for him. He and Alice planned to work in Africa together for the next couple of years. After that, they had agreed they would try for a baby.

Alice's father had been a little wary of Dante at first but as soon as he'd met him again, the two men had hit it off. Dante was a match for her father in every way and now there was healthy respect between them. Her father had been surprised when Alice had shared her plans about using most of her inheritance to fund her work in Africa. Seeing that she was resolute and knowing that there was nothing he could do to dissuade her, eventually he had given in. To top off her happiness, Alice had learned through Linda that they had managed to locate Bruno's remaining family in one of the other camps, a grandmother and aunt. Although distraught that Bruno's mother was dead, they were overjoyed to find that her child was alive and had come to take him home at the first opportunity. Alice planned to visit Bruno when she and Dante next returned to Africa.

Now, finally, it was their wedding day.

They were to be married in the Piazza della Signoria, where they had met, before going back to Dante's family home in the mountains for the reception. Dante's mother had refused to have the wedding feast anywhere else and had been cooking for days.

As Alice stood beside her husband-to-be, in the red room of what passed for Florence's city hall, she glanced around. All her family was there, and his too—as well as those of the staff from the camp who could take the time off. She slid a glance at Dante, who looked every inch the proud Italian. Life with this man would never be easy, but it would be exciting and filled with joy.

'I love you, *tesoro mio*,' she whispered as the room hushed.

He slipped an arm around her waist. 'I know it, and I love you.' His eyes darkened. 'I promise you that every day will be happier than the one before.'

They stood side by side, as Alice knew they would throughout their lives, as at last they were pronounced man and wife.

* * * * *

Mills & Boon® Large Print Medical

November

HER LITTLE SECRET	Carol Marinelli
THE DOCTOR'S DAMSEL IN DISTRESS	Janice Lynn
THE TAMING OF DR ALEX DRAYCOTT	Joanna Neil
THE MAN BEHIND THE BADGE	Sharon Archer
ST PIRAN'S: TINY MIRACLE TWINS	Maggie Kingsley
MAVERICK IN THE ER	Jessica Matthews

December

FLIRTING WITH THE SOCIETY DOCTOR	Janice Lynn
WHEN ONE NIGHT ISN'T ENOUGH	Wendy S. Marcus
MELTING THE ARGENTINE DOCTOR'S HEART	Meredith Webber
SMALL TOWN MARRIAGE MIRACLE	Jennifer Taylor
ST PIRAN'S: PRINCE ON THE CHILDREN'S WARD	Sarah Morgan
HARRY ST CLAIR: ROGUE OR DOCTOR?	Fiona McArthur

January

THE PLAYBOY OF HARLEY STREET	Anne Fraser
DOCTOR ON THE RED CARPET	Anne Fraser
JUST ONE LAST NIGHT…	Amy Andrews
SUDDENLY SINGLE SOPHIE	Leonie Knight
THE DOCTOR & THE RUNAWAY HEIRESS	Marion Lennox
THE SURGEON SHE NEVER FORGOT	Melanie Milburne

Mills & Boon® Large Print
Medical

February

CAREER GIRL IN THE COUNTRY	Fiona Lowe
THE DOCTOR'S REASON TO STAY	Dianne Drake
WEDDING ON THE BABY WARD	Lucy Clark
SPECIAL CARE BABY MIRACLE	Lucy Clark
THE TORTURED REBEL	Alison Roberts
DATING DR DELICIOUS	Laura Iding

March

CORT MASON – DR DELECTABLE	Carol Marinelli
SURVIVAL GUIDE TO DATING YOUR BOSS	Fiona McArthur
RETURN OF THE MAVERICK	Sue MacKay
IT STARTED WITH A PREGNANCY	Scarlet Wilson
ITALIAN DOCTOR, NO STRINGS ATTACHED	Kate Hardy
MIRACLE TIMES TWO	Josie Metcalfe

April

BREAKING HER NO-DATES RULE	Emily Forbes
WAKING UP WITH DR OFF-LIMITS	Amy Andrews
TEMPTED BY DR DAISY	Caroline Anderson
THE FIANCÉE HE CAN'T FORGET	Caroline Anderson
A COTSWOLD CHRISTMAS BRIDE	Joanna Neil
ALL SHE WANTS FOR CHRISTMAS	Annie Claydon